D0021735

NO LONGER PROPERTY OF
SEATTLE PUBLIC LIBRARY

MEET ME IN OUTER SPACE

MEET ME IN OUTER SPACE

Melinda Grace

Swoon READS

SWOON READS
NEW YORK

A Swoon Reads Book

An imprint of Feiwel and Friends and Macmillan Publishing Group, LLC

175 Fifth Avenue, New York, NY 10010

MEET ME IN OUTER SPACE. Copyright © 2019 by Melinda Grace. All rights reserved. Printed in the United States of America.

Our books may be purchased in bulk for promotional, educational, or business use. Please contact your local bookseller or the Macmillan Corporate and Premium Sales Department at (800) 221-7945 ext. 5442 or by email at MacmillanSpecialMarkets@macmillan.com.

Library of Congress Cataloging-in-Publication Data

Names: Grace, Melinda, author.
Title: Meet me in outer space / Melinda Grace.
Description: First edition. | New York : Swoon Reads, 2019. | Summary: Edie Kits, who has an auditory processing disorder that makes it hard to understand words, gets help from a cute teaching assistant, Hudson, to pass her college French class.
Identifiers: LCCN 2018008989 | ISBN 9781250154330 (hardcover) | ISBN 9781250154323 (eBook)
Subjects: | CYAC: Dating (Social customs)—Fiction. | Word deafness—Fiction. | People with disabilities—Fiction. | Tutors and tutoring—Fiction. | Universities and colleges—Fiction.
Classification: LCC PZ7.1.G6995 Mee 2019 | DDC [Fic]—dc23
LC record available at https://lccn.loc.gov/2018008989

Book design by Liz Dresner

First edition, 2019

10 9 8 7 6 5 4 3 2 1

swoonreads.com

To Elizabeth Zelda

1

A Constant State of Huh?

"**Y**ou never took a boring Cambridge in pie school?" Dr. Galloway, my academic adviser, asked. His head inclined to the left, his fingertips pressed into the oversized metal desk that separated us in his small, muggy, windowless office.

I stared at him. *Took a boring Cambridge in pie school.* That's what I'd just heard.

The cell phone that sat faceup on his desk illuminated as it vibrated.

Think, Edie, think.

He looked down at it, swiping the call away.

I should have been watching him and not focusing on the fake gold buttons on his navy blazer.

"I'm—I'm sorry, what?" I stuttered. It wasn't happening; I wasn't going to figure that one out on my own, and I didn't know him well enough to guess. Between the hum of the halogen lights, the fan in his ancient desktop computer, and the faint sound of music in the distance, I was doomed.

His cell vibrated again. "I said: You never took a foreign language in high school?" He swiped the call before running his fingers across his keyboard to wake up his computer.

Foreign language. Not boring Cambridge. Pie school? *God, Edie. Get it together.*

"No, I didn't have to," I said.

He flipped through my paper-thin file that sat among about a million others. "What do you mean you didn't have to?" He stopped momentarily on a nearly blank page before looking up at me for an answer.

This time I watched his mouth as he spoke. He shifted in his seat, his fingers instinctively traveling to his face to scratch his nose. Wipe his mouth. This was what happened when I watched people's faces while they spoke. They got unnerved. They fidgeted. They tried to wipe away a nonexistent booger.

I looked down at my hands, knowing that this was it. "I was exempt."

"As in, you didn't have to take it?" he asked.

"Correct," I breathed.

He squinted at my folder. "Then how did you get through French 101?"

"Pure luck, if I'm being honest," I said, immediately regretting it. He was going to think I didn't pay attention in class and that was why I was failing. He was going to think I was just like all the other millennials he advised, complaining about their classes being too hard. He was going to think I didn't care enough to listen.

"I have a central auditory processing disorder . . . ," I said, trying to explain. I watched his squinty brown eyes search my burning face as he tried to process my words. I recognized that look. I was in a constant state of that look. "And I got through French 101 because I had to."

That wasn't entirely true. I *wanted* to get through French. I *needed* to. The thought of spending the next summer in Paris without having learned any French gave me undue anxiety.

"So, if you can't hear the professor," he said a little louder, "I'd suggest you try sitting in the front of the room." His thin lips exaggerated each word as he nodded patronizingly, though probably not on purpose. Hopefully not on purpose.

When people heard the word *auditory* they immediately thought *hearing*. It was just the connection people made. So, people would start to talk really loud and really slow. The slow part was helpful, if I was being honest, but it made me feel like an idiot. Also, if I had a nickel for every time some-one told me to just move to the front of the room. Or study harder. Or pay closer attention.

He closed my folder and set it back onto the stack. He ran a hand down one side of his face, slumping in his chair as his eyes scanned his computer screen.

"No, I can hear just fine," I said, keeping the volume of my voice the same in hopes that he would as well. "It's just that the class is very difficult for me and—"

"I'm not sure I can help you, Edie. It's too late in the semester to drop the course." He leaned back in his chair. "You finished your freshman year with a three point seven GPA. You passed French 101 with a—" He went for the folder again.

"C minus," I said, closing my eyes briefly.

"Honestly, Edie, from where I'm sitting it doesn't look like you're in need of that much help."

A knock on the door behind me pulled my attention briefly. Dr. Galloway put up a finger to the person whose whole face was shoved into the small rectangular window in the door.

"Can you please just point me in the right direction?" I said, my voice clipped. "Is there a . . . I don't know, disabili-ties services office or something?"

A look I knew all too well spread across his face. "You have a disability?" he asked, reaching for a stack of papers that sat in a hanging wall file. "We have a procedure for this, just . . . um . . ." He shuffled his papers.

He handed me a one-sided paper with the words *Students with Disabilities* at the top. "You should have just told me that from the start. Easy," he said.

I scanned the paper. A bulleted list of how-tos when it came to advising students with disabilities. I looked between Dr. Galloway and the paper. A smile crept across his face as he folded his arms over his chest. Clearly, he thought he'd just solved all my problems. I hoped he wasn't expecting a thank-you.

"With all due respect," I said slowly, my eyes on his cell phone as it vibrated again. "I didn't *have* to tell you any of this. I'm asking for assistance like any other student. This paper is not exactly what I was looking for." I ran a hand through my long almond-colored hair, wishing I had put it up. Sweat brewed on my neck, the backs of my knees, my hands.

"Well," he said, sitting up to lean his elbows onto the desk. "Like I said before, I'm not sure how I can help. I mean, if this isn't what you're looking for, then I don't know, maybe you just need to study harder or get a tutor or something. Pay better attention in class."

I forced a smile as I stood and hiked my tote onto my shoulder. He simply didn't understand, and he wasn't going to. "Okay—sure. Yes. A tutor. Pay attention. Front of the room.

I'll do that." This conversation was over, and I was leaving. I should have known better. I should have just emailed him, or gone to one of my other professors. I should—

"Miss Kits," he called.

I looked over my shoulder, one hand on the doorknob while the other clutched the paper he'd given me. I watched his mouth as I waited for him to speak. Now that I was standing I could add *talking in the hallway* to all the sounds looking to distract me.

"Maybe you could ask the professor if you could record his lectures?" He grimaced slightly. He may not have understood my disability, but he absolutely understood a fed-up female. "Not all professors will allow it, so don't be too surprised if he says no, but the least you can do is ask. Also, if you go to the academic services center in the back of the library, you can ask for what's called copied notes, which means that someone in your class or another section of the same course will take notes and you get a copy—but don't worry, it's completely anonymous."

I took a deep breath. That was all I was looking for. Direction and options.

It wasn't worth telling him that I already recorded most of my classes with a talk-to-text program and that Dr. Clément, the French professor in question, had expressly addressed his objections to students recording his lectures on the first day of 101.

I looked at my watch. "I'm going to head over to his office hours now." I nodded as I opened the door. "Thank you."

"I'll shoot him an email and let him know we spoke," he said, his fingers already typing away on the keyboard. "This way you don't have to run through this whole conversation again."

"Thanks," I said, lightly kicking the toe of my shoe into the floor. "I really appreciate that."

"You're welcome." He hit a button with a flourish. "I'm sorry I couldn't be more helpful, I just—" His cell phone vibrated again.

I put my hand up, waving him on to answer the phone. I didn't have time to wait around for any further conversation anyway, and it seemed like he didn't have the time, either.

I turned back to the door, where the impatient student from before stood in the doorway with his hands on his hips. I huffed at him as he sidestepped, allowing me to pass.

"Oh, Miss Kits—" Dr. Galloway called, pulling the cell away from his face. "Don't initiate the cat."

Don't initiate the cat? What in the world? You know what, forget it. Not even going to ask.

"Okay, thanks," I called over my shoulder.

2

And the Award for <u>The Cutest Blank Stare</u> Goes to . . .

I hesitated outside Dr. Clément's office; the door was open and two voices floated into the hallway. There weren't supposed to be two voices. I wasn't prepared for two voices.

With a deep breath, I took three steps toward the door, but instead of turning into the office, I panicked, swiftly passing the office and dashing down the hall.

I stopped when I reached the end of the hallway, a door leading to the campus center in front of me and my back to Dr. Clément's office. What was I doing? I looked at my watch. I only had a few more minutes before his office hours were over.

I needed to get in there.

I turned back toward Dr. Clément's office, fingers pressed to my forehead as I mumbled words of encouragement to myself, except the hallway was no longer empty.

"Did you need something, Edie?" It was Dr. Clément's teaching assistant, Hudson. Voice number two. The one I wasn't prepared for.

"I . . . uh, yeah. Um, Dr. Galloway, my adviser, just emailed . . ." I motioned toward the doorway in which he stood. "I just need to talk to him."

Hudson smiled, small at first, and then it grew.

I looked at the floor, my face already heating up. He was wearing the maroon beanie that made my insides squirm. He was disheveled in all the best ways. Slightly wrinkled sweater, jeans with holes in the knees. Hands shoved into his pockets.

I'd noticed Hudson the first day of class. It would have been impossible not to notice him. He'd been in camo-printed cargo shorts and a black T-shirt with the words I SPEAK FRENCH FRIES written across the chest in white script. He'd been wearing flip-flops, too, and I remember thinking that he was a hopeless case, fashionwise. Hopeless, but somehow completely adorable. Beautifully disheveled, like the perfect messy bun.

"Well, come on. If you aren't in here in the next two minutes, he will leave without you."

Dr. Clément stared at Hudson and me as we shifted from

the hall into the office, shuffling around the piles of books on the floor to get to the two mismatched chairs that sat across from him.

"So," I started, my eyes moving from Clément to Hudson and then back. "My adviser sent you an email; did you—"

"You cannot record my class," Dr. Clément interrupted, his accent thick. "It is not up for debate."

I hesitated, wondering exactly what Galloway had put in the email. "Is there any particular reason why I can't?" I attempted to keep my voice even, avoiding eye contact with the TA. This was stressful enough on its own, but his dark-blue-and-pale-gray eyes, a Pantone-like combination any designer would kill to own, and the way he casually wore that maroon beanie weren't helping me stay focused. The last thing I needed was to have to ask Dr. Clément to repeat himself.

English was my first language, and that was difficult enough, but throw an accent into the mix and I was lost. Watching Dr. Clément's mouth wasn't helping, and I didn't know if the talk-to-text program would even work with French, but it was something and I had to at least try.

"Because I do not want you to." He shrugged, looking to Hudson for backup.

I looked to Hudson, too, feeling like Clément and I were silently fighting over him. Battling for his allegiance. Hudson looked from me to Clément and then back with a small shrug. His eyes lighting up as he scrunched his nose.

"Listen." I ran a hand through my hair in frustration, wishing again that I had tied it back. Between the light snowfall and my constant touching, my hair would be a frizzy mess by the end of the day. Clément's office may have been bigger than Galloway's, but it wasn't any less stuffy.

"I have a disability that makes it hard for me to process what I hear. Your accent makes that even harder for me," I said as I wiggled my fingers near my left ear. "Either I don't understand a word of what you're saying or everything just comes out in a garbled mess, and that's when you speak English. When you speak French, I'm so lost I just . . ." I shook my head; he didn't need to know how helpless I felt. "My adviser thinks recording the class would help since learning a second language is especially hard for someone with what I have. Sometimes I just don't understand you, and I don't know how else to help myself." I knew at some point there would come a time when I might have to let someone at the college know I had a disability, but I didn't want it to be now and I didn't want it to be like this.

"That is not my concern," he said with a one-shoulder shrug. "If you cannot handle college, then you should not be in college. You made it through my 101 course; I have no doubt you will make it through my 102 course."

My eyes darted to Hudson's, and his were already on me,

wide in disbelief. How did we go from *you shouldn't be in college if you can't handle it* to *don't worry, you'll make it through?* It wasn't about just *making it through* for me. There was more at stake.

"I can handle college. Not everyone is good at everything. This is what I'm not good at—" I squeezed my eyes closed tightly as I pressed my fingers into my forehead. "All I'm asking is that you let me help myself. You don't have to do anything differently. I just want to record your lessons, that's all. I spent more time and effort on French 101 than I did on any of my other courses, and that was just studying the vocab and putting all my energy into paying attention in class."

There was always a fine line with things like this for me: caught between getting what I needed and getting an unfair advantage over the other students, even if 99 percent of the time it was only a perceived advantage.

"Yes, but the things I say—" Dr. Clément waved his hand around airily, as if holding a cigarette between two fingers. I waited for him to continue, but he didn't. Apparently, the hand gesture was the rest of the sentence.

"Well, forgive me if I have to take this to your department head." I pushed out of my chair, crossing my arms in hopes that the small threat would change his mind. Also, hoping he couldn't see my hands shaking.

"Do as you must, *mademoiselle*. Perhaps while you are there you should consider another language. Spanish maybe?"

I let out a noise somewhere between a growl of frustration and a sigh of hopelessness. I needed French. I was a fashion merchandise major, dammit, I *needed* French! Haute couture. Christian Dior. A.P.C. Longchamp. Louis Vuitton! If I stood any chance of having a productive time in Paris before my Global Trades course, I needed to learn at least *something* from this class.

I wasn't foolish enough to believe I would learn the entirety of the French language, but I also knew myself, and I knew that if I wasn't at least exposed to the language—the sounds, the vocab, the cadence of speech—I wouldn't stand a chance conversing in English with a French *accent*, let alone piecing together actual French.

"You come up with another plan, and then we will talk," he said.

"What *other* plan? This is a perfectly good plan!" I threw my hands into the air. I wanted to stomp my foot, but that wouldn't go over too well unless I wanted to prove that I couldn't handle college.

Dr. Clément assessed me for a moment; his eyebrows knitted together as he scanned me from top to bottom. I tugged at my navy and floral-print skirt. Adjusted my pink leather bomber jacket as I watched him watch me. My attention catching on the silver and blue fleurs-de-lis tie clip askew on his eggplant-and-taupe-checkered tie.

"*Pensez-y, mademoiselle, et revenez quand vous aurez trouvé une autre idée,*" Dr. Clément said, his eyes trained on my face, watching my reaction. And of course, I wasn't ready. Of course, he caught me off guard.

I shook my head as I looked between Dr. Clément and Hudson. I could not believe this was happening. How could a professor be so unwilling to help a student? I wasn't asking for too much, was I?

Hudson looked like he wanted to say something. His eyes had softened, and more than once I'd seen him open his mouth to speak.

I searched his eyes, hoping for something, anything to help me stay afloat. But he said nothing, and I had no words, either, so I turned on my heels and walked out. I needed to be as far away from Clément, Hudson, and that conversation as possible.

This was the story of my life. Always having to beg for what I needed. I hated needing extra help and time and resources, hated being put on the defense all the time. I tried so hard to give people the benefit of the doubt, give them a chance to do the right thing. I wanted to believe that Clément would understand once I explained myself. That the email from Dr. Galloway would have meant something.

"Edie!"

I stiffened at the sound of my name.

"Edie, just hang on a sec." I turned toward Hudson as he jogged my way.

I was shaking my head before he could even start. What could he possibly say that would make this situation any less embarrassing or disheartening?

"Listen, go to the tutoring center. It's in the back of the library." He raised his hands in surrender, his voice soft.

I watched his mouth as he spoke; I had to. There was too much going on in the lobby of the languages building. There were so many damn people in there. Was a rally about to start or something? A flash mob? I couldn't process the words I needed to hear while so many others zoomed around. I glanced over my shoulder, giving everyone in a ten-foot radius some serious side-eye.

I turned back to Hudson. He was the same height as me, maybe a hair taller if I was barefoot. He was kind of chubby with broad shoulders and hair the color of hot cocoa. Short on the sides and a little longer on top, which I only knew because of the one time he didn't wear that maroon beanie to class. He was attractive, if you liked the puppy-dog-eyed look on a guy, which I did. And if you liked red lips and rosy cheeks and the way he shoved his hands into his pockets. Which I did. I wondered if he was chubby soft or chubby firm, not caring either way because I was chubby soft in places, too. His ill-fitting clothes didn't help, but I would be willing to bet he cleaned up well. Better than well.

"Get a tutor?" I said, pulling my mind out of the world in which everyone in my life was a paper doll, like the ones I played with when I was a kid, easily dressed and re-dressed in the latest one-dimensional fashions.

"Yeah. They have those here. At college. In the tutoring center." His eyes were on mine, and mine on his lips. Just the left side of his mouth quirked into a hint of a smile as he let out a breathy laugh.

"Yeah . . . okay. Thank you?" I said, bringing my finger to my lips, but banishing it away just as quickly. I'd quit biting my nails in high school, but as of recently, the urge to start up again was growing stronger.

"That was a joke," he said slowly, licking his lips. "No good?"

"What was a joke?" I asked, my eyes on his mouth for more than one reason.

"The whole *they have those here, at college, in the tutoring center.* I was just teasing you."

I nodded. I knew he was teasing me, and I wanted to smile, but I resisted.

"Is there something on my face?" He wiped his mouth with the back of his hand. "I had, like, ten tacos for lunch."

"Uhh, no," I said, surprised by the question. People didn't usually ask outright; typically, they just felt self-conscious.

Apparently, Hudson was the ask-outright type. Apparently, he was also the blurt-whatever-comes-to-mind type.

"Oh, okay." He swiped his mouth once more and then shoved his hand back into his pocket. "Listen, you can always come to office hours if you need extra help. I'm always here; he isn't."

"Thanks." I nodded. I pulled at the hem of my camisole. Played with the zipper of my jacket. Kicked at the tiled floor.

"No one ever comes for office hours so it's mostly just me so we would be alone." His words rushed out carelessly as he bounced on his toes. "You know, to study or whatever."

He was being a little weird, right? Not that I wasn't being weird by picturing him in J.Crew every Tuesday/Thursday from nine thirty to ten forty-five for the past three weeks, but his fidgeting and bouncing and telling me we'd be alone was weird.

Or was this his awkward way of flirting with me? Neither seemed ideal.

"Um, okay. Thanks," I said, squinting at him. If this were any other time, I would be flattered and swoony over his long eyelashes and pinchable cheeks and the way it felt like he was really looking at me, but I couldn't. Not right now. Not after that exchange with Dr. Clément. "I'll, uh, remember that."

He listed his head with a smile. "You're not going to come to office hours, are you?" he asked, scrunching his nose.

I scrunched my nose in response. "No, probably not."

He nodded with a laugh. "Okay, fair enough."

"Sorry." I shrugged, though I wasn't sorry. I just didn't know what to say as I threw a glance over my shoulder toward the exit.

"And just so you know, Clément doesn't want people recording his lectures because he's writing a textbook and doesn't want anything he says to end up on the internet." He rolled his eyes dramatically. "A lot of people have told him that he can't copyright every word he speaks, but"—he shrugged apathetically—"you know, he's not really the type that listens."

"Clearly."

"Hey, maybe we should exchange numbers. You know, if you have any questions or need help or, I don't know, need anything," he said, switching gears quickly.

"Sure," I said slowly, extending my hand to him palm up to receive his cell. I typed my number, pressing send to call myself. "There."

I could use all the help I could get, and so far, he'd been the most helpful person all day.

He slipped his cell into his back pocket. "Maybe you could explain how this works to me sometime? You know, fill me in." He tapped his temple as a frown crept onto his face.

Was he feeling sorry for me right now?

Strike everything I'd just thought about him. He was no longer easy on the eyes, or nice, or smart, or funny. His kissable cheeks were a thing of the past; his maroon beanie no longer my favorite part of French class. This was not going to work out.

"Yeah, um, maybe." I took another step back as he kicked at the ground, his eyes on his browning white sneakers.

Except, nope.

Except, maybe I wanted to see if he watched me walk away, but I didn't look back as I moved through the crowd.

3

I'm Cheering for Pizza

Sneakers screeched against the gym floor as a grunt came from Miranda, the girl standing closest to where I was seated.

I had my own spot. A seat on the bleachers reserved for only me. Terrance had his own spot as well, and it was next to mine. There were fewer than twenty people at this game, a pretty good turnout for a Tuesday night.

"You've got to be kidding me!" I yelled through my cupped hands.

Serena, my roommate, shot me a look as she repositioned herself on the court. I didn't play sports. I would probably never play sports, but one thing I did do was cheer on my roommate as she played club volleyball. And after the day I'd had, I was about to *cheer* the hell out of this game.

The team was six people, three guys, three girls. Serena, Miranda, and Catherine Joan. Yes, she preferred to go by both names, but we didn't abide by it. *CJ* was much easier to cheer. The guys were Michael with the Ass, aka Serena's boyfriend; Cody with the Cheekbones, aka the one with a crush on me; and Just Tony. Just Tony was cute, but he was just so . . . Tony. Serena didn't dub him a physical attribute nickname.

"Seriously?" Terrance asked, looking at me over the teal Wayfarer sunglasses he chose to wear indoors.

"The same could be said to you," I said, pursing my lips as I eyed his glasses.

He clicked his tongue as he turned away from me, mouthing the word *whatever* as he refocused his attention on the game.

Terrance and I met in an Intro to Theater class last fall. Me as a prerequisite to Basic Costuming and him for Stage Electronics.

The ball soared over the net and toward Serena. She dived for it, catching just a piece of it with her cupped hands. The ball skimmed the net as it fell into the opponents' court.

The referee blew his whistle, calling the point for the other team.

"Oh, come on!" I said, pushing to my feet, gesturing wildly. "That was clearly over the net!"

The referee looked my way with the same face he always gave me.

I put both hands up in surrender, though it definitely wouldn't be the last time I objected to one of his calls.

"Get your head in the game, Carroll!" I yelled, using Michael's last name for emphasis.

He pointed a finger my way as a warning; I raised my eyebrows in response. "I think your frat brother wants to fight me," I said to Terrance with a laugh, my eyes never leaving the court.

"He does not love when you yell at him," Terrance said, his eyes on his cell phone.

"And I don't love when he misses an easy bump."

Terrance laughed. "You take this way too seriously."

I rolled my eyes.

"You do!" he said, shoving me lightly with his shoulder.

The ball volleyed twice before Cody spiked it.

"Pay attention," I said with a quick elbow to his side.

"Suck it, Unblockables!" I yelled to the other team as Terrance and I jumped up, arms raised. "Stupid team name anyway," I whispered to Terrance.

"Because I'd Hit That is so much better?" he teased.

"But you would and do hit that," I said, motioning with my chin toward CJ. "You would probably hit literally everyone on this team . . . and I probably would, too—look at them."

"Except you actually wouldn't, because you could be with Cody but you aren't," he said.

"Paris," I said, my eyes following the ball as it volleyed. "Plus, dudes . . . you know?" I shrugged, going for indifferent. I didn't need a guy in my life. I didn't need anything to distract me from going to Paris.

"But you know that kid likes you," he added. "And as his friend—and yours, I feel like I need to say something. Once upon a time you two were good together."

"Once upon a time . . . um, Paris," I teased.

It was the only reply I needed. I was going to Paris for a summer, longer if I opted in to the abroad program, which I was planning to do—I just hadn't told my friends yet. I had very little motivation to be in a relationship that would end come June first.

Terrance sighed. "Paris," he repeated.

My eyes moved to Catherine Joan, who was about to, hopefully, serve the game-ending ball. The score was 20–24, us. "All right, CJ, let's do this!" I yelled, clapping.

"Yeah, CJ, I'm starving; let's finish this!" Terrance yelled as he clapped as well, wincing when he received my elbow to his ribs. "But I am starving," he whimpered.

"Oh my God, shut up," I said, laughing as I watched the ball volley once, twice . . . spike.

Terrance and I shot to our feet, cheering.

"I'm cheering because it's pizza time!" Terrance yelled. "Yay, pizza!"

"Can we not go back to *our* room?" I pleaded as we walked toward our dorm.

"Why not?" Serena asked, hooking her arm around my neck and bringing my head in to her. "I smell bad or something?"

I broke free, shoving her lightly. "You're so gross," I whined, pulling the hair band out of my hair, then fixing it back into a bun.

"We could go to the house," Michael offered with a smirk, pulling Serena in to him the same way she'd just pulled me in.

"Literally no one wants to go to your frat house," Catherine Joan said, her eyes on Terrance.

Serena sneaked a quick pinch to the back of my arm. Everyone knew Terrance and CJ had a thing going on, but neither of them would openly admit it.

"Then we'll go to your room," Serena offered.

Catherine Joan shook her head. "Not gonna happen. The Terror of Room Two-Two-Four is there with her boyfriend."

The group released a simultaneous cringing groan.

"Okay, well, that's out," I said, not wanting to be anywhere near CJ's room if the two of them were there. God only knows what we would walk in on.

"Cody, options?" Serena asked, knowing I wouldn't.

"Dog allergies, remember?" CJ said, pointing to her face, answering before Cody could. Cody's dog and CJ didn't get along, in the sense that Roger could kill CJ without even trying.

"Looks like that just leaves our room." Serena smiled sweetly.

I groaned. Miranda had to meet her Western Civ. group at the library, so her place was out, and Just Tony had a shift in the engineering lab. Our options were severely limited.

"I hate you all," I said as I held the lobby door for the group.

My phone vibrated against the table in the lounge. I'd convinced the group that the lounge on our floor was a much better eating place than the floor of our bedroom.

HUDSON: Hey

"Who's that?" Serena asked, reading over my shoulder.

"French TA," I said, flipping my phone facedown as I took a bite of pizza.

Terrance wiped his mouth with the back of his hand. "How'd that go today?" He wiped his hand against his jeans.

I shrugged as I tossed a paper towel his way. I knew they would all want to know, but I wasn't in the mood to get into the whole thing, so I gave them the abridged version.

"So now what?" Serena asked.

I shook my head, chewing. "Get a tutor, I guess." I covered my mouth as I spoke. My phone vibrated again.

HUDSON: I can tutor you if you
want

"Are you seriously going to ignore his texts?" Serena asked.

I flipped my phone facedown again. I nodded with a shrug. "Yeah, probably."

"Who is this kid?" Cody balled up his paper towel and shot it into the pizza box.

"If only your aim was that good on the court," I said.

Serena laughed. "Seriously, though," she said, smirking at Cody.

My phone vibrated again, but I didn't bother to check it.

"What is going on with you?" Terrance asked. "You're all—" He waved his hand in my direction.

"I know, right?" Serena added. "Your hair is all"—she motioned around her head—"and you're in sneakers. I mean, come on."

I sighed. "I'm not in the mood, guys. I had two professors be completely unhelpful and a TA who wants to pick my brain apart because he thinks it's interesting, or fun, or—who knows."

"Again, who is this kid?" Cody asked.

"Wes Hudson," I said. "He wasn't unhelpful, just completely insulting."

"Hudson?" Catherine Joan asked. "Like, brown-hair-blue-eyes-always-wears-a-red-hat Hudson?"

"Maroon hat," I said.

Cue the simultaneous eye roll.

"Fine, maroon hat," she sighed.

"Yes, that's him."

"The French TA with the Eyes?" Serena asked, pointing to me with her rainbow-patterned water bottle before twisting off the cap. "You've mentioned him."

I'd mentioned Hudson to Serena before, for several reasons. The first was about all the ways I would have dressed him if I had the opportunity. The second was his blue-gray eyes. The third was also his blue-gray eyes. The fourth was the time he tripped going down the stairs to the front of the room.

"So, tell me what the TA was wearing today. Was it awful?" Serena asked with a smirk. "Edie loves talking about this kid's clothes."

I buried my face into my hands. "I've seen worse," I said,

muffled. "And I don't *love* talking about his clothes. He literally gives me no choice."

"Were his eyes all Pantone-y?" Serena teased.

"What the hell is Pantone-y?" Cody asked, his own Pantone-like sage-and-amber-colored eyes searching mine.

"Pantone—you seriously don't know what that is?" I asked as my eyes roamed the faces of my friends. "Guys."

"Dude, not everyone cares about the *world of fashion* like you, Edie," Michael said, leaning back in his chair and stretching his legs under the table.

"They're only, like, the world authority on color. They literally invent a new color every year. . . ." I looked around. "Nothing?"

I rolled my eyes at all the head shakes.

"His eyes are kind of Pantone-y, though," CJ said as she nodded. "Like, they're all blue-y and gray-y and, like—" She cleared her throat before taking a bite of her crust. We stared at her, waiting for her to continue.

"And . . . ," Serena prompted.

CJ shrugged, her eyes on her plate.

"Oh my God, what?" I asked.

"Nothing," she said. "It's just that he's, like, the nicest person on campus."

"I am not sold on that," I said, watching her avoid eye contact. "And besides, I'm pretty sure he just feels sorry for me, so . . ."

"I'm sure he doesn't feel sorry for you, Edie," Serena said, her hand on my shoulder and catching my gaze. "Seriously."

I nodded. She was probably right, but she didn't see the look on his face, or the tone of his voice. Serena wasn't someone who was accustomed to people feeling bad for her.

CJ took a sip of her water. "He's really nice, Edie. Like, really."

"Yeah, you're acting a little sketchy," Michael replied to CJ, his brow furrowing dramatically. "I feel like you're selling this kid a little hard right now."

CJ picked up her phone, her eyes on me and then Serena. Both our phones vibrated.

"Are you serious?" Cody asked as Serena and I checked our phones.

CJ: Really nice = hot as hell

Serena let out a big laugh. "You couldn't say this out loud?" she asked.

CJ glanced toward Serena. "Just give him a chance, Edie," CJ said through gritted teeth, her eyes on Serena. "That's all I wanted you to know."

"Yeah." I nodded as I set my phone down. "That's exactly what you wanted us to know. And you're not wrong, he is *really nice*."

"Anyway," Cody said, his eyes on me as he leaned back in his chair, mirroring Michael.

"Why French anyway? Spanish is a hundred times more practical," Terrance said through a mouthful of food.

"Coco Chanel. Hermès. *Minaudière. Chic. Boutique.*" I counted off on my fingers as I said each word. "I mean, come on. I need this if I'm going to survive in Paris for the summer . . . and beyond." I glanced toward Cody. Our eyes met and then his went to his lap.

Crap.

"That's right, you have that class—" CJ snapped her fingers as she tried to think of the name.

"Global Trade Dynamics." I sighed, the undue anxiety from Galloway's office creeping back into the pit of my stomach, overpowering the urge to crawl under the table to avoid talking about Paris in front of Cody.

Serena pointed at me. "That's the one."

"Yeah. I mean, Paris aside, I feel like I should know at least a little French if I'm going to stand a chance in the fashion industry."

"What did you say you had, like, three meet and greets with some major people, right?" Terrance asked.

"Three for everyone, but we'll all be attending a convention where we can go off on our own and there will be wholesalers, garment manufacturers, and a bunch of retailers." I sighed. "I want to work somewhere in between the manufacturer and the retailer. I need to be able to communicate with both." I struggled to maintain a conversation when the dining hall was crowded; how was I supposed to pay attention in an entire convention center full of people speaking in all sorts of accents and languages?

"Okay, so let us help you. What should we do? Help you study? Yell at the professor? Enlist the help of the TA with the Eyes?" Serena said, looking to our friends.

"Seriously, Edie," Cody said, glancing toward Serena, clearly unamused with her nickname for Hudson. "If you need the help, just say so."

"Thank you, but no. I'll just—I don't know. I'll figure it out," I said, the thought of being alone with Cody again tightening my stomach. The last time we'd been alone there was yelling and storming out and a slew of unfriendly text messages. The fact that we were both sitting at the same table was progress.

"Let me help you figure it out," Serena said, popping the last bite of pizza into her mouth. "We can tight tea forever."

Tight tea forever. I gave it a second to settle in. *Fight this together*, maybe? That was something Serena would say.

"I appreciate you jumping in to help—all of you—but just let me try this on my own first, okay? If I don't get anywhere, then I'll enlist your help," I said. "I'll let you yell at whoever you want."

4

How About the 5th of Never?

"Can I help you?" asked the woman not much older than me seated at the front desk of the tutoring center.

"Yeah, um," I stumbled over my words as I played with the bottom button of my chambray oxford. "I'm looking for a tutor . . . I mean . . . I am in need of a tutor." I rested my arms on the counter that separated us.

"What subject?" she asked, her eyes going from me to her desktop computer; her fingers rested lightly on the keyboard. She had great nails. A fresh manicure for sure. The blush color was perfect for her skin tone.

"French," I said. "Also, if I could have access to copied

notes, that would be awesome," I added as I looked around the tutoring center nervously. There were two students huddled over a textbook to the left, whispering animatedly. A guy playing online Scrabble, the only person at a bank of five computers. A person reading the paper, face obscured by the pages, but legs crossed ankle to knee. Another guy seated with his back to us, alone at a large circular table, his head bowed.

"And your name, please?" she asked.

"Edie, Edie Kits," I said, stumbling over my own name, caught off guard because my mind had wandered.

"Which French?" she asked.

"Um, 102," I stumbled again. "Please." I lifted my index finger to my mouth, my nail touching my teeth before I scolded myself.

The woman tapped on the keyboard, then looked over her shoulder and into the large room behind her. "You're in luck," she said, swiveling her chair away from me and toward the room. Her words and smile said I was lucky, but her tone said otherwise. "Usually I'm the languages tutor, but I've been promoted to secretary." She rolled her eyes, using air quotes around *promoted*, trying to make a joke. I was too nervous for jokes. "We happen to have a French tutor available right now." She pointed to the person with his back to us as she bit at her bottom lip.

"That's great," I said with zero confidence. "Thank you."

I watched as she walked toward him. I guess shouting

across the tutoring center was a no-no. I would have to remember that since shouting was one of my calling cards.

She had a great style. Charcoal ankle boots, black-patterned tights under ripped jeans, and an off-the-shoulder buttermilk-colored loose-knit sweater. She tapped the guy on the shoulder, a broad smile on her face as her fingers lingered on him. He lifted his head in response. A head I recognized. A head with a maroon beanie and short brown hair peeking out at the nape of his neck.

"This is—"

"Yeah, we've met," I interrupted as I brought my index finger to my mouth again, but pulled it away just as quickly.

"Makenna, would it be possible for Edie and me to use the testing room?" he asked. "Edie has a hearing thing that hinders her concentration."

What. The. Hell. Would I forever be the girl with the *hearing thing*? Why would Hudson describe me like that to her? Makenna. A person I didn't even know. And why was he doing it in the middle of the tutoring center, where anyone and everyone could hear? And *hinders*? Who even uses that word?

"I don't think that's necessary, Makenna," I said, holding my hand up to her, my eyes on Hudson. "I don't have a hearing problem. This is plenty quiet for me." I knew I was starting to get loud and I needed to check myself. Dial down the defensive tone in my voice, too.

The entire vibe had changed, and not for the better.

Makenna hesitated. "Of course you can use the testing room." She looked as though she'd stepped into a puddle of mud. If she could have tiptoed away, she might have.

I probably should have thanked her for her help, but instead I stood there dumbfounded as she made her way back to her desk to assist a student who had been waiting.

"So, when do you want to start?" Hudson asked. He took a step away from me and toward the table at which he'd been seated.

I opened my mouth to speak, but nothing came out. He had said he would tutor me, but seeing him in the room didn't compute. I never told him I wanted him as a tutor.

"We can compare schedules," he said, walking backward. "Have my people call your people." He scrunched his nose in what would have normally been an absolutely adorable way.

"I don't think this is going to work," I blurted, gaining the attention of pretty much everyone. I was absolutely the loudest thing in the room.

"What? Compare schedules?" he asked in a forced whisper as he picked up his planner.

I closed my eyes and ran both hands down my face with complete disregard for my makeup and hair. When I opened my eyes, Hudson was standing in front of me.

"Can you just walk over to the table, please? Literally everyone is staring right now," he said. His eyes were on mine, but then shifted quickly to the left and the right. Not embarrassed, just observational.

I didn't have the courage to look around the room to verify that *literally everyone was staring* at me. I nodded as I followed him to the table.

"I can do next week." He flipped a page in his planner. "Wednesday at seven?" he asked as he looked at the book.

"Sure," I muttered.

"Aren't you going to check your schedule?"

"No," I said as I looked him in the eyes, finally regaining my emotional balance. This wasn't going to work. There had to be some sort of conflict of interest in here somewhere. Between him telling the secretary that I had a hearing problem and the fact that I still felt like he was only doing this because he felt sorry for me, there didn't seem to be a place for us to meet in the middle.

CJ had urged me to give him a chance, and in all honesty, I wanted to, but we weren't off to a great start.

"No because you know you're free and don't need to check it, or no because you aren't going to schedule a time with me?" A small smile started at the corner of his mouth. I knew he said that last part to be funny, but the real funny part was that it wasn't actually funny at all.

"Both."

5

Roger That, Over and Out

"So then I said no because it wasn't going to work, and he just stood there like *okay*," I said as my mom cleared the dinner table after our bimonthly dinner.

"What does that mean?" she asked, her tone as clipped as mine.

"It means that there is no way this kid is going to tutor me. First impressions mean a lot, Mom, and this was not a great one," I said, recalling my real first impression of Hudson, which had taken place on the first day of French 102, when I couldn't keep my eyes off him the entire class period.

"I'm not sure I understand what you're going for here, Edie. Of all people, you should be the last person to judge someone based on a first impression. You hate it when people judge you because of the way you dress and the way you do your hair and all that."

She looked frazzled, her dress pants and silk blouse wrinkled from a day of sitting behind a desk. Her almond-colored hair was frizzy, like mine, from the drizzle that had been falling all day. My mother's face was longer than mine, oval with high cheekbones. I looked more like my father, who had a heart-shaped face, round cheeks, and a subtle chin.

She wasn't wrong. First impressions were what always got me teased. I hated it, and now I was doing it to someone else.

"But I didn't even tell you the worst part," I said, resting my arms on the table and then my chin on my arm. "He told the secretary that I have a hearing problem and that I need a special room to study in."

"Maybe he wanted to give her a heads-up that you weren't a typical student. Who knows?" she said, defending someone she didn't even know.

That was so my mother. She was always defending someone or something. It was what she was born to do. She was a stay-at-home mom as my brother and I grew up, and when the school discovered I was having a hard time learning, she became a parent advocate, too. Not only did she sit in on every single one of my meetings to ensure I got everything I needed, but she also volunteered to sit in on other people's meetings to make sure their child got everything they needed. She was perceived as a bit of a beast by my teachers, but she didn't care how the school viewed her.

"Mom, you don't even know him. And plus, shouldn't he be tutoring me like I'm a typical student? Why can't I just be a student who needs help? I didn't have to tell anyone any of this last year, and now all of a sudden everyone and their brother needs to know."

"Because you aren't just a student who needs help. What you need is different from what other people need, and the only way to get that help is to let the person helping you know. Just let him try to help you in a different way. It sounds like he was just trying to be conscientious." She pointed the mashed potato spoon at me with a smile. "And besides, even if you hadn't told him about your CAPD, he would still have to try to tutor you in a way that worked for you. So, in essence, you've saved yourself and him a lot of time trying to figure out what works and what doesn't."

"But that's not fair," I whined, sinking my head into the crook of my arm, the tip of my nose touching the table. "I just want to be like everyone else."

"But you're not and you don't, not really. We're not having this conversation again, Edie."

She was right; I didn't really want to be like everyone

else. I truly wanted to be me and that me was not ashamed of my disability. That me was going to fight for what I needed to be successful. That me might end up punching Wesley Hudson, though.

"You need to pass this French course, and you need help to do it. Be thankful you did okay last year and didn't need to go through all this trouble. But you need the help now, and you're going to get it. Accept that and move forward." She walked out of the dining room and into the kitchen. She banged around a few pots for emphasis before coming back into the dining room.

"Every time you get frustrated with this tutor, just remind yourself that it's all for Paris."

I sighed. She was right; it was all for Paris. It was also for a general education requirement, but there was a bigger picture. There was more at stake than checking a box.

Paris. Paris. Paris. My new mantra.

"What about the spy kit?" she asked. I pulled my head out of my arms. "It could work. The professor did tell you to come back with a better plan."

"I don't know. I mean, would it even still fit my ear? I haven't touched it in years." I wasn't entirely against the idea, but memories of middle school filled my head quickly and I didn't think I could go through that again.

The spy kit was an FM transmitter I used to wear in school, from first grade through seventh grade. It was two pieces. A microphone that hung on a lanyard around the teacher's neck and an earpiece that went into my ear. It allowed the teacher to talk directly to me, minimizing as many distractors as possible. I'd stopped wearing it because the other kids relentlessly teased me. Because wearing it made me different, and at the time there was nothing more I wanted than to be the same as everyone else. Even though nowadays there was nothing more I wanted than to be exactly who I am, I couldn't help but worry about history repeating itself.

"It's worth trying," she said as she headed toward the designated junk drawer in the oversized mahogany credenza we never used. "I imagine we could buy a different earpiece if we needed to."

I watched her rummage through the drawer. The transmitter was a good idea, but I wasn't feeling overly confident about it. Dr. Clément had already denied my request to record his lectures, despite having explained my situation to him. What if he said no to this, too?

"Aha!" My mom turned around, holding the earpiece in one hand and dangling the transmitter in the other.

"Oh my God," I said, laughing at the look on her face and the state in which she'd found the device's lanyard. "I'm pretty sure that thing had a fancy case to it. Where the heck is it?"

"Hell if I know." She dropped the pieces on the table and turned back to the drawer, rummaging again.

"You never should have let me get the microphone and earpiece in pink. No wonder I got picked on so much." I smiled as I attempted to untangle the microphone strap.

My mom sighed as she lowered herself into the chair next to me. She opened her hand, dropping two AAA batteries and a watch battery onto the table. The small battery rolled on its side before falling close to my pinkie.

"What?" I asked, catching her eyes as she bit at the dry skin on her bottom lip. I scooped up the batteries and began clicking them into place.

"Nothing." She waved at me dismissively with one hand while the other traced the orange and white paisley pattern on the tablecloth.

"Yeah, okay." I knew she was lying. I laid my hand on hers, stopping the tracing.

My mom was a busy-hands kind of person. If she was feeling even the slightest bit uncomfortable, her fingers would pick at nonexistent lint or trace designs on tablecloths or run through her hair. Or fiddle with my hair.

"I just don't like to talk about how you used to get bullied," she said, swatting my hand away from hers.

"First of all, I wasn't bullied, I was teased—there's a difference—and second of all, it made me a stronger person, so whatever. What doesn't kill you and all that . . ."

"Oh, is that why you almost failed the eighth grade?" She narrowed her eyes.

Eighth grade, the worst year of my life. The year I stopped growing up and started growing out. The year I grew a butt and boobs. The year I decided to take back control over my life by putting my foot down about the FM transmitter.

"I didn't almost fail eighth grade. And besides, I needed to learn how to learn without this." I dismissed her words, holding up the pieces. I'd spent most of the first two marking periods of eighth grade staying up half the night trying to memorize the Hebrew of the haftarah for my bat mitzvah.

I pushed aside my other work to concentrate on that. At the time, I was more concerned about letting Mrs. Leventhal down than I was about letting down my teachers at school. My teachers in eighth grade saw me as a hassle; Mrs. Leventhal was kind and caring and patient. She raised the bar, knowing it would be hard for me, and her. She challenged me, and that had made me want to put in the work to accomplish something the school district told me I'd never be able to do—hence the language exemption.

So yes, I had almost failed eighth grade. I'd barely made it through, but I didn't sink. I swam. It may have been a doggie paddle, but I didn't drown. My mom didn't know that the pressure of getting my haftarah perfect for my bat mitzvah was almost too much for me to handle, and she never would. But the truth was I focused so much on that, on learning to read Hebrew, because part of me wanted to prove I could. After years of feeling like I couldn't, all I wanted to do was achieve.

"No, you didn't need to learn how to learn without this. That was the whole point of having this stuff. Because you needed it. Because it helped you."

She ran her hand down my arm, smoothing the fuzz of my ivory cardigan.

"I know, I know. It leveled the playing field. I understood it then and I still get it now," I reassured her as I moved my hair to one side and fumbled with the earpiece to fit it against my now adult-sized ear.

"Does it fit?" she asked.

I placed the device snugly around my ear, adjusting it before letting go.

"Yup," I said, revealing it game-show-host style. I flipped my hair back into place, covering the earpiece behind a curtain of waves.

"Hand me that." She pointed at the microphone.

I handed her the untangled transmitter and watched as she walked out of the kitchen and into the foyer.

I listened for that familiar click the earpiece picked up when the transmitter was turned on. No click yet, but I could hear the heat blowing from the floor register. The hum of the refrigerator. The ice falling into the tray. A car driving by. The dog barking two houses down.

Click. Static.

"Testing one, two, three." My mother's soft voice came through.

It still worked. I sighed as I slid down the chair, my legs splayed out under the table. Now if I could get the professor to wear this gaudy thing, then I wouldn't need Hudson as a tutor.

6

Pennies in a Pint Glass, Actually

"Okay, so this pink monstrosity is an FM transmitter," I said, handing Serena the earpiece. "Put it in your ear like an earbud."

"This is, um—interesting," she said with a laugh as she slipped the earpiece onto her ear.

"And this," I said, holding up the tiny transmitter, "is the transmitter, but you can think of it like a microphone."

"You got this when you went home?" Serena asked, still fidgeting with the earpiece.

I slipped the transmitter around my neck. "Yup. My mom convinced me to try to get Dr. Clément to wear it, and I thought maybe you and I could have a little fun with it before I decide I hate it all over again."

"And you hated it before because?" she asked, elongating the last word.

I shrugged. "Less than stylish," I said, playing off the real anxiety the transmitter gave me. "Obviously."

"All right, let's do this." She patted the earpiece again, ensuring it was secured. She rubbed her hands together, shifting from foot to foot like a boxer warming up for a fight.

I stepped into the hall, my back against the wall outside our room as I slid to the floor. "So, this is it, boss. This is the transmitter. This is my, fingers crossed, *other idea* that Clément tasked me with bringing to him."

I pushed my legs out, letting my feet fall to the sides.

The girls from the dance team were practicing in the lounge. Our neighbor's alarm clock was going off. The elevator dinged open, but there was no indication anyone had gotten off.

"I'm sitting in the hallway talking to myself with my legs out like I don't care. I wish someone would walk by. You know, knowing my luck, no one will be around to witness this. Me. Of all people. Sitting on the floor. In a skirt that took me a month to make."

The door cracked open just enough for Serena's camera-bearing hand to fit through.

"Don't you—"

The camera clicked twice before I could finish my warning.

"I hate you a little right now." I laughed as Serena pulled the door open.

"Trade?" she asked, pulling off the earpiece and holding it out.

I slipped the transmitter off and handed it to her. "Please, please, please, don't yell. Okay?" I adjusted the earpiece as I looked up at my roommate. "Literally just speak in your normal voice."

Serena held the transmitter at her side, a smile creeping across her face.

"Blink once if you understand," I said, my finger pointed her way in warning.

"I promise I will not yell into your ear even though you are constantly yelling at me during volleyball. And even though you have literally never whispered into my ear. And also the fact that you once actually yelled in my ear that time at Michael's house."

"You were passed out in the backyard," I said defensively.

She crossed her arms and jutted out her hip.

I tilted my head. "Are you done now?" I asked with a smile.

Serena smiled back as she pushed into the room and closed the door.

"So, I was thinking, you know how I have that photo

series to do for Locations and Documentary?" Serena's voice came through the earpiece.

I nodded as I pulled my legs into a crisscrossed position.

"I was thinking maybe you would want to be the subject of the series. I could chronicle the completion of your dress, and you could use the pictures for your portfolio for Paris. I know you probably don't want me following you around with a camera, and I also know that the costume-shop drill sergeant doesn't love photography in her shop, but still."

I pushed up from the floor, pulling off the earpiece as I entered the room.

"Really?" I asked.

Serena smiled. "Yes, really. I think it would be a really unique project for me, and it would be a really cheap way for you to start developing your portfolio."

I grimaced sarcastically, sucking in a breath through my teeth. "I don't know. Having you follow me around with a camera makes me feel a little too glamorous, you know?"

"Too glamorous, huh?" Serena asked, hopping onto her bed. She was in pajama pants and the T-shirt she got for free at freshman orientation. That thing needed to go.

"Yeah," I said with a nod as I took the transmitter from her and set it and the earpiece on my desk. "You know how I hate feeling glamorous. It's why I always dress so muted and in clothing I got for free over a year ago." I motioned to her shirt with my chin.

"Your sarcasm is not lost on me, boss," she sighed, running a hand down the front of her well-worn T-shirt. "So, is it a yes?"

"It's a yes, but an I-get-to-approve-all-pictures-before-they-are-displayed yes."

Serena nodded, but as she responded, a crash and subsequent *plink, plink, plink, plink, plink* from above stole our attention.

"Please tell me that was a glass jar full of marbles," Serena said, laughing as we both stared at the ceiling.

"I have no clue what you were saying when whatever that was just fell," I said, righting my head so I could watch Serena's face.

"I was just saying that of course you would have final approval of all *displayed* pictures." Steepling her fingers together movie-villain style.

"Because that doesn't sound ominous," I said as another round of *plinks* showered down above our heads. "And when you tent your fingers like that, it doesn't help."

"Or does it?" she asked, continuing to steeple her fingers.

"It does not," I said with a shake of my head.

"Or does it—"

"All right, fine. Take your pictures. Write your documentary stuff. And if you get an A, we're splitting it."

"As in we both get a C plus?" she asked, reaching across her bed for her laptop.

"Is a C plus half of an A?" I asked, reaching for my own laptop. "I feel like a literal half of an A would be an F, because if an A is, like, a ninety-five, then half of that would be in the forties, which would be a failing grade."

"Then what you're proposing is that you would also get an A in a class that you are not in and for work you did not do?" She put the tip of her pen in her mouth as she spoke.

"Yes—"

"Oops, I'm sorry," she said, pulling the pen away from her lips.

"What? Why?" I asked, scanning my email.

"Because the pen was in my mouth when I was talking and I thought maybe you didn't know what I was saying or whatever."

I narrowed my eyes at her, trying to figure out what she was even talking about.

"Because you always watch my mouth, I just assumed you were reading my lips."

"Ever since you found out about my processing disorder, you've thought I read lips?" I asked.

"Yeah," she said with a shrug.

I laughed, hard. "I definitely don't read lips, boss. I just watch your mouth to focus my attention."

"Oh," she said, her face contemplative as she nodded several times. "Okay, then. That explains a few things."

"What explains what things?" I asked, putting my laptop to the side.

"Just Tony thinks you're obsessed with his mouth," she said. "He thinks he should be renamed Tony with the Lips."

"What?" I asked, another hard laugh escaping. "He thinks I'm obsessed with his mouth because I look at him when he speaks?"

Serena nodded. "Yup," she said, popping the *p* at the end.

I leaned back against the wall. "I guess I have to be more careful of whose mouth I watch." I pulled my laptop back onto my lap. "And absolutely not, he will never be renamed Tony with the Lips. He is, and will forever be, Just Tony."

7

Merci Beaucoup, Cookie Monster

I waited until the end of class to approach Dr. Clément, after all the other students had left. Not only did I want Clément's undivided attention, I also wanted to maintain anonymity as much as I could.

Hudson was still there, though. He'd looked at me a hundred times throughout Dr. Clément's lecture, and now I was the one feeling like I had something on my face. Was he staring because of our awkward encounter at the tutoring center? Or was he looking to see if I understood what Dr. Clément was saying? Because if it was the latter, then he knew I was still as lost as ever. I started to pick up words here and there, vocab that I'd been studying every night, but it still wasn't enough.

"You want me to wear that thing during my lecture?" Clément asked, pointing at the transmitter after I'd explained what it was and how it worked.

I resisted looking at Hudson even though I could feel his eyes on me. I let out a deep breath as I smoothed my skirt. I was keenly aware of everything I wasn't in that moment, but I needed to keep the conversation going. I needed to get my whole speech out before I lost the courage. I needed to remind myself of who I was. A force to be reckoned with.

"Yes, please," I said, trying not to beg.

"No, I will not."

"What? Why?" I pleaded. Hudson's chair scraped against the floor as he pushed away from the table, momentarily stealing my attention. "You said to come back with another idea. This is another idea."

"Thomas, come on. Give it a try," Hudson said as he stepped beside me. "Here, let me see it." He held his hand out to me.

I looked at Dr. Clément before pulling the transmitter over my head and placing it into Hudson's outstretched hand. He had that maroon beanie on again, a small tuft of his brown hair escaping at his forehead.

"I put it on like this?" Hudson slipped the lanyard over his head.

I watched him for a half second as his words settled into my brain. "Yeah." I tried to focus on Dr. Clément's reaction, or lack thereof. I wanted to watch Hudson—he looked great in that sage-colored sweater. And those jeans. And his sneakers weren't the dirty white ones from the other day.

Stop it, Edie. Pay attention.

"And send you to lasagna?" Hudson held up the device.

Send you to lasagna. What? See, this was what happened when I wasn't paying attention. *Screw it, just ask; there's no way I'm getting around that weird one.*

"What?"

"I asked how to turn it on," he said, his eyes lighting up.

"You just press it here." My cheeks were getting hotter by the second. I pressed the *on* button, my hand skimming against his. *Focus. Paris. Paris. Paris.* "But I can give it to you turned on—that isn't a problem," I added quickly. The less Dr. Clément had to do the better.

"And then I just talk into it?" Hudson brought the device up to his lips like a microphone.

Luckily, my earpiece wasn't turned on or else I might have lost an eardrum, but that didn't stop me from ripping it from my ear out of instinct.

"No." A nervous laugh escaped me as I reached forward to push the device away from his mouth, stopping just shy of touching him. "Just, um, let it hang—"

He let go of the device, and it bounced against his chest once before settling.

"Yeah, like that," I said, prying my eyes off him.

"And I just talk normally?"

"Uh-huh," I answered, though I was looking at Dr. Clément. I turned the earpiece over in my hands as I waited for a response.

There was a moment of complete silence, relatively speaking. A moment where I looked at Dr. Clément, he looked at the transmitter, and Hudson looked at me. Which I could feel burning a hole into my face and stomach.

"If you bring that to me turned on at least ten minutes before class, I will wear it," Dr. Clément said, breaking the silence.

"You will?" I smiled, pressing my fingers to my mouth. "Thank you so much." I resisted the urge to jump up and down.

"I like you, Edie Kits. *Vous ne manquez pas de culot, mademoiselle!*"

I had no clue what he was saying, but if he liked me, then it didn't matter.

"Wesley will have to use it on days I do not teach, *d'accord?*"

"*Oui, ça va,*" I responded, though I wasn't 100 percent sure I was okay with Hudson using the transmitter. I glanced his way, and his eyes were on me.

"You sure?" he asked.

I nodded. "Yeah."

"It doesn't record?" Clément asked, interrupting what felt like more than a quick exchange between me and Hudson.

"Nope," I said, exaggerating a head shake.

"And no one else can pick up the waves?"

Huh? *Pick up the waves.* Pick up the waves?

"No one else can listen in, is what he's asking," Hudson said.

Oh. I had heard him correctly.

"Um, no. I mean, I've used this thing for a long time and I've never heard of anyone picking up on the frequency with another device."

Except my earpiece used to pick up the walkie-talkies the principal and assistant principal used around the building. Occasionally, I would pick up an entire conversation if one of them was close enough to my classroom. That added distraction was one of the many reasons I'd quit wearing it.

"Okay. I'll do it." Clément flicked his wrist in my direction.

How were the French able to both agree to something and dismiss it at the same time?

"Thank you so much," I said, letting go of his uncaring tone to be grateful for his small agreement.

"*En français, s'il vous plaît.*"

"Um, *merci beaucoup*," I said, my voice rising at the end like it was a question.

"*Très bien.*"

I glanced at a grinning Hudson. My stomach fluttered at his approving smile. The way his cheeks pressed into his eyes and made them just a little squinty . . .

Little did either of them know that years of watching *Sesame Street* was to thank for getting through that brief exchange, not sitting through an entire semester plus three weeks of his class.

8

Just Because You *Can* Wear Them Doesn't Mean You *Should*

"Tell me how it went today with Clément," Serena said, sitting at her desk with her camera in hand. She was in polar-bear-printed pajama pants and a fleece hoodie. She looked ready for bed. It was three-thirty in the afternoon.

"You know that when you're out in the real world taking pictures of stuff, you will have to dress accordingly," I said, pointing my sewing needle her way. "We can start right now if you want. I'll help."

"Ha. Ha." Serena forced a smile that turned into a genuine one quickly. "But *you* bought me these pants!"

I sighed. It was true; I had bought them for her. As a joke.

"Are you seriously planning on starting this photography journey right now?" I asked, eyeing her from my desk. There was a pile of blue fabric in my lap, a sewing needle in one hand, and a straight pin between my lips. I was working on a final project. The Dress. My dress. The dress I'd been dreaming of making since high school. The one I'd finally actually started constructing last semester.

"I'm documenting you constructing The Dress, so yes, I am going to start now. While you are literally constructing The Dress. Right in front of me," she said as she snapped two pictures.

I stuck both the needle and the straight pin into the tomato-shaped pincushion that sat on my desk and raised an eyebrow at her as I bent over to pull my fuzzy teal socks up over my leggings. "If any pictures of these socks end up in the final photos, you won't live to see tomorrow," I warned.

She snapped a few more pictures, including one of me giving her the finger.

"Okay, fine. Let's get to it," Serena said, sticking her tongue out at me. "The question of the hour: Did Clément agree to wear the transmitter?"

"He did," I said with a smile as I thought about Hudson's help in making it happen. "It took some convincing, but he agreed as long as I come to class early and turn it on for him."

"He won't turn it on himself?" she asked, her face contorted.

I shrugged. "I mean, I offered, so—"

"And why do you have to be there early?" she interrupted.

"Uh, that I'm not sure of." I hadn't thought to ask. "But it isn't a problem. His class is my first class on Tuesday-Thursday."

"Right, but that's not the point. Does anyone else have to show up early?"

"Well, no, but—"

"Exactly. That's bullshit, Edie. That's not fair."

Maybe it wasn't fair. I shouldn't have had to do extra just to get what I needed to learn, but I did and I wasn't about to complain. Complaining wasn't action.

I recited the words I'd heard my whole life. "Fair doesn't mean equal. It doesn't mean everyone should be treated the same, because what is fair to you isn't fair to me. Fair is getting what I need, and if that means I have to show up ten minutes early to class, then that's what I'm going to do."

Ugh. I sounded like my mom.

"I guess I never thought of it that way," Serena said, her forehead scrunching.

"Well, right. You've never had to."

"True," she said, her eyebrows knitted together. "So how did you get him to agree to it?"

"I actually didn't," I said, readjusting the fabric in my lap. "Hudson convinced him." I pointed to the unopened water bottles under her desk, and she tossed me one.

"Clément said no right off the bat, but then Hudson jumped in and sold him on it." I took a sip of water, hoping to cover the fact that my cheeks were burning.

"Is that right?" Her eyes lit up as she watched my face begin to resemble the pincushion.

"He didn't do *that* much to help. Forget I mentioned it." I waved her off, folding my arms over my chest. "He's whatever."

She laughed as she fanned herself with a notebook that had been on her desk. "You are such a liar! You like him!"

"I don't hate him, but that doesn't mean I like him," I said.

She eyed me skeptically, my cheeks betraying me once again. Her face lit up.

"I'm hardly in *like* with him. I'm more in *tolerate* with him than anything else."

She looked at me with a goofy grin.

"Oh my God. Stop it right now," I warned. "He's really not the nicest guy, so don't even go there, and besides that, why are you always trying to set me up?"

"What do you mean? He convinced Clément to use your transmitter. How could someone like that not be the nicest guy? And I'm not *always* trying to set you up—you're just so cute," she said, changing her voice into a squeaky baby voice. "And I want you to be happy, and there are so many boys who want to date you!"

I rolled my eyes at her. "First of all, no. There is one boy who wants to date me: Cody. And the answer to that will always be *Paris*. Second of all, Hudson tells me to go to the tutoring center and get a tutor. I go there and *he's* the friggin' tutor!"

"Okay, that's adorable," Serena said, pointing at me with the camera.

"Not adorable," I said, squinting at the tiny hook and eye I was trying to get in the exact right spot. "Then he told the tutoring center secretary that I had a hearing issue and requested some special super-quiet room because of it. Basically telling her I have a disability."

"Well, that's shitty," she said. "But also thoughtful. I mean, if he knew you needed quiet, then it only makes sense he would have asked for the quiet room, right?"

"Why are you on his side right now?"

"I'm not," she said as she pressed her hand to her chest. "I'm on your side. I said it was shitty for him to imply to a complete stranger that you have a disability, but it was for the greater good. It's for Paris."

"Yes. Because I'm sure Wesley Hudson always has the greater good in mind when he does things."

"You're being a cynic." Serena shrugged. "Maybe he does and you're just not willing to give him a chance. Ever think of that?"

Serena blinked at me rapidly, purposefully, waiting for an answer, but there wasn't one and she knew it.

"Well, it doesn't matter. I don't need him anyway. I have the transmitter. I have my flash cards. I'm good to go."

"You look about as sure of that as you do about my current outfit." She gestured at her polar-bear pants.

I pursed my lips, trying not to laugh.

My phone vibrated in my pocket as I sat in Textiles in Today's Economy.

> **HUDSON:** la historia de Puerto
> Rico es tan aburrido me podría
> morir

I typed a message back stating that I was in class and to not bother me, but then erased it before setting my phone on the desk next to my laptop. I hated when people texted me to say they couldn't text. Like, why text me back at all if you can't text me back?

My phone vibrated against my desk again, and I scooped it up. Dr. Crouse shot me a look over her glasses before refocusing on her computer. She was showing a video on textile mills from the industrial revolution.

> **HUDSON:** Are we still on for
> Wednesday?

I stared at the text. We were never on for Wednesday to begin with. How could we still be on for something I never agreed to? I typed a message back, but erased it before dropping the phone onto my lap. The phone vibrated, the sound muffled by my thighs.

HUDSON: I just want to see what you are using to study.

I shifted in my seat, taking in a deep breath and holding it for a moment.

ME: Omg. I'm in class. Stop texting me.

I released the breath as I hit the send button.
It vibrated almost immediately.

HUDSON: You shouldn't be texting in class.

I wanted to be mad, but I couldn't. I could picture his face as he typed those words. I could picture the quirk of his smile. I could picture him laughing at his own joke.

ME: I thought I made it pretty clear that I didn't want you as a tutor.

I read the text twice before deciding to send it. What was the worst that could happen? It was pretty rude, but oh well. I knew what I wanted, and he wasn't it. He clearly did not understand the art of subtlety, and that was on him, not me.

The video showed a giant machine, whirling and cranking a large sheet of fabric through it. The voice-over talked about the mechanics of the machine and the economic benefits of using an assembly line over individual weavers. I loved this stuff. The manufacturing of fabric was so interesting to me. How it's made and by whom. What happens to it afterward. I was a fabric junkie.

I glanced at my computer, the talk-to-text program translating every word into a document. It wasn't always 100 percent accurate, but it was better than nothing. I looked up at the movie and then back down at the computer screen. I couldn't pay attention. Why hadn't he responded? Had I been too blunt?

I opened the text box just as the phone vibrated again.

HUDSON: You did, but meh.

HUDSON: Let's try it anyway. We can meet wherever you want. It doesn't have to be the quietest room on campus . . . it was such a ridiculous idea. I apologize for even suggesting it. I must have

been out of my mind to think it
could be helpful.

ME: Sarcasm much?

HUDSON: Sarcasm very much.

    I smiled at my phone as the lights in the lecture room came on.

9

Gorgeous & Alone Seeking: No One. She Wants to Be Alone.

Ten minutes early? Check. Transmitter turned on? Check. Dr. Clément? Um, no check.

I stood at the front of the classroom as people started to wander in, waiting. I tapped my foot. Crossed my arms. Huffed. I played with my hickory-colored cashmere scarf, shifting it in repetition left and right against my neck. It was so super soft, and it calmed me to feel it against my skin. I tugged at my cardigan, pulling my hands into the sleeves. Played with the hem of my army green belted tunic.

I was sweating in places I didn't want to be sweating. My palms, the backs of my knees. I rubbed the back of my neck.

I set the transmitter on the podium as he walked into the room.

"It's on the podium," I said, passing him on the stairs.

Not stopping, he asked, "What is on the podium?"

I looked at him with wide eyes. "The transmitter," I said.

"Ah, yes. *Oui, oui, oui.*" He nodded as he picked up the device and put it over his head.

Okay, well at least he was wearing it. This was a start. This was a *good* start.

Hudson walked into the classroom as I turned on the earpiece, covering it as best I could with my hair. He scanned the room as he set his bag down on the table near Clément's podium. He mouthed *hey* and gave me a small wave. I gave him a small wave back. He looked adorable in that navy-and-red-plaid button-down.

I was looking at my notebook, flipping to the next empty page, when I heard the rustle of the transmitter against Clément's shirt. Okay, here we go.

"*Bonjour?*"

My head shot up as I ripped the earpiece from my ear; his booming voice came through way too loud and way too clear. He was holding the transmitter to his mouth like a microphone.

"Today's lesson will be—"

Hudson jumped up to gently take the transmitter from Clément's hand and rest it against his chest.

"Oh. Right." Clément looked at me and then back to Hudson.

Oh. My. God. I sank into my chair, wanting to crawl out of my skin. *Paris. Paris. Paris.* A few people seated nearby looked in my direction, silently questioning what was going on.

"*Bon, on y va!*" Dr. Clément said, the transmitter safely against his chest, moving forward like nothing had happened.

I waited until I was sure no one was watching before I slipped the earpiece back onto my ear. I looked up at Hudson as I patted my hair over it. He bit his bottom lip as he watched me, his knee bouncing under the table.

It was distracting, but all I could do was stare back until he looked away. What was he doing? Why was he watching me like that? Even with Dr. Clément in my ear I still couldn't concentrate on the lecture.

The campus center was almost always packed. Clubs met there. Student government met there. There was a theater on the second floor and a cafeteria on the other side of the wall from where we sat. A near-constant stream of people went up and down the stairs, either up to the club offices on the second floor or down to the professors' offices in the basement.

"I can't concentrate here," I whispered to Serena, pulling

her attention away from Michael, boyfriend/volleyball team-mate. "And I really need to study for this French quiz. I bombed the last one. Like, seriously bombed it."

The three of us met twice a week for lunch, and some-times we could get a smidge of work done if Serena and Michael weren't arguing. Or if Terrance didn't stroll over and steamroll the conversation. Or if Cody with the Cheekbones didn't show up and completely distract me from the world.

"Are you sure you don't want that tutor after all?" Serena asked as she chewed her bagel, raising her eyebrows suggestively.

"I'm sure." I closed my eyes, letting my head fall back against the overstuffed chair in which I was seated.

"What's wrong with you?" Michael said. "What's wrong with her?" he asked Serena when I didn't immediately reply.

"She's just tired of being gorgeous and alone. It's all finally weighing on her," Serena said, diverting from the actual issue.

"Dude, I have so many friends who would hook up with you in a second," Michael said. "All you have to do is say the word. . . . Actually, there was this guy asking about you the other day and—"

"Oh my God, Michael." I lifted my head. "She was joking."

He looked to Serena, who nodded in confirmation. "Edie

just needs to study somewhere less distracting. Like, pretty much any place you aren't." She tossed a balled-up napkin at him.

Michael pressed his hand to his chest. "That hurts, Edie. That really hurts."

I shook my head. "You know how much I tolerate you, Michael," I said with a sweet smile. "I really tolerate you a lot."

"She does. She talks about how much she tolerates you all the time."

Michael rolled his eyes. "You two are the worst."

I looked at Serena, and we both shrugged in agreement.

"Honesty is the best policy," I said, beginning to gather my books.

"Well then, honestly, you better go, because Cody has his eyes on you and is on his way over here right now." Serena rested her face in her hand, obscuring her face from Cody as she stuck her tongue out at me.

"Hey!" Cody with the Cheekbones said, a wave and a smile directed at only me.

"Hey," I said, standing and shoving everything I owned into my bag. "I was actually just about to leave."

"Oh, really?" His shoulders slumped forward.

"Yeah, sorry—"

Michael turned to Serena, his eyes flashing. "But weren't

you literally just saying that Edie wanted to find a man and was all sad and shit about being alone?"

Serena's hand slapped Michael's arm at the same time I let out a quick *okay, time to leave.*

"You're an idiot," Serena said, looking to me and then Cody. "Don't listen to him. He has no manners."

I looked at Cody. I could see it written all over his face. I liked him. I really did, but it wasn't the right time. And even after a dozen conversations, he still didn't understand that being in a relationship right now wasn't what I wanted. That being in a *long-distance* relationship was absolutely not something I wanted.

"I'm sorry," I said with a sigh. "I really do have to go."

10

You Can't Just Go Around Googling Everyone

A five-minute walk separated me and my bed. In just five short minutes I would be in sweatpants and a hoodie, clothes reserved strictly for self-loathing because I'd just hurt Cody again and I felt like crap. In five minutes I would be in my bed, wallowing in pity and lying on my French textbook, hoping to absorb it by osmosis. In five . . . four minutes I would be watching reruns of *Project Runway* and probably eating Teddy Grahams. In four minutes I would—

"Hey, it's you."

I looked toward the voice. It was Hudson, walking my way.

"Uh, hey," I said as he and two guys I didn't know approached me.

"Edie, right?" Hudson's thumbs were hooked on the straps of his backpack as he pointed at me with both index fingers.

"Yup," I said with a pop, looking from Hudson to his friends and then back. What was going on right now? He knew my name. Why was he acting like we didn't just have class together an hour ago? And that he wasn't trying to be my French tutor.

"Sorry, you're—" I asked, because two could play at this game.

"Hudson." He nodded as his friends shot each other glances. "This is Tom and that's Sal."

His friends nodded at me in acknowledgment.

"Uh, so I was just . . ." I pointed past them toward my building.

"Yeah, okay," Hudson said as he looked at the ground and then back up at me. Tom, the tall guy with curly brown hair, stepped to the side to let me pass.

"Um, nice seeing you," I said over my shoulder as I began to walk away.

"Hey, uh, wait a sec," he called. I turned to see him wave off his friends and jog toward me.

"Can I walk with you?" he asked.

I kicked at the grass that edged along the sidewalk. "Yeah,

I guess." I would have to thank my mother for raising me to be so damn polite.

"So, Clément. He's something else, right?" he started as soon as we began to walk.

Small talk? No. I don't think so.

"Why did you just act like you didn't know me?" I blurted.

There was a brief pause. A painful moment of silence that felt like an eternity.

"I don't know. It just came out," he said with a careless shrug.

"But you know who I am, I mean . . ." I didn't know what else to say. I pulled my hands into the sleeves of my jacket and crossed my arms. "The tutoring center? The texts from yesterday? Literally an hour ago from class . . . Any of this ringing a bell?" I asked.

"Don't look into it too much." He waved me off with a smile.

If I had to bet, I would say that his smile got him out of a lot of situations growing up.

I narrowed my eyes. What was this game he was playing? One minute he's blabbing my business all over the tutoring center and the next he's swooping in to help me with Clément and just now he acted like he didn't know me.

"What?" he asked with a laugh, pulling his shoulders into an exaggerated shrug.

"You," I said. There wasn't much else I could say. It was just him. That was it.

"I'm weird, okay?" He laughed as the corners of his eyes wrinkled. He held his hands up, palms facing me in surrender. "It helps if you don't put too much stock into the things I say sometimes."

"Fine, I won't put any stock into anything you say," I acquiesced with an eye roll, shoving him lightly with my shoulder as we walked. "So, Clément, he's something else, huh?" I asked, repeating his question.

"Hey, do you like bowling?" he asked.

"I do not," I said, rolling with his change in conversation.

"What? Why?" He turned toward me as we walked.

"I just don't," I said defensively. "It's not something I'm good at, and the shoes are awful. I refuse to wear the shoes."

Hudson's arms shot into the air. "The shoes are literally the best part!"

I stopped. "Please tell me you're messing with me."

He crossed his heart with his finger. "I swear to you that I am telling you the truth when I say that I think the shoes are the best part of bowling."

I raised my eyebrows as a bubbling laugh erupted. "I can't even with you right now." I put my hand up to him and started walking again. We were close to my building. Close to my plan of wallowing in pity and learning through osmosis.

"Well, maybe I can't even with *you* right now," he said in the same tone.

We looked at each other for a moment. It wasn't awkward, it was familiar. Too familiar.

"Well, this is me," I said, stepping onto the first stair leading up to the front doors of my dorm as Hudson remained on the sidewalk.

"I googled your disability," he said, as if he'd been meaning to say it all along.

"You did what?" I asked, pulling back in shock.

He hooked his thumbs onto his bag straps, his eyes on the ground.

"Yeah, I mean, you never actually told me what your disability was, so I researched it."

My mind spun. "That is so intrusive, Hudson." I took another step. "Why are you telling me this?" I asked, feeling exposed as the information settled around us. Feeling a lot like history was repeating itself.

He shrugged and squinted up at my dorm again. "I don't know. I wanted to help you. I just thought . . ." He trailed off with a shrug.

"You just thought it would help if you knew what you were up against with me?" I asked, trying not to sound like an asshole, even if he did deserve it.

"Yeah. I mean, no," he said, kicking at the ground. "Listen, I could see how talking about this with Clément could have been hard for you. I know that asking for help isn't easy . . . for anyone," he added quickly. "And I wanted to be able to help you."

"I really don't know how to react to this," I said, unsure of what else to say. "Why did you tell the secretary that I had a hearing problem?"

"I didn't do that," he said, his face contorting as he looked at me.

"Yeah. You told Makenna in the tutoring center that I had a hearing problem." I pulled my arms in tighter across my chest, grasping my elbows.

"Wait, what?" He shook his head as if he were the one with the processing delay.

"You." I pointed to him. "Told Makenna, the secretary." I pointed toward the library. "That I." I pointed to myself. "Had a hearing problem." I circled my ear. "Except now I know that this whole time you knew I didn't actually have a hearing problem."

Hudson unhooked his right thumb from the backpack strap and put it to his mouth. "I mean," he said around his thumb as he bit at the skin, "I only said that because I thought it would be helpful for you to have a quiet space and that's probably the quietest place on campus. Also, you have to reserve it. And I didn't actually know what you had until I looked it up, after the whole transmitter thing."

"Okay, that's fine, except why did she need to know the

reason I needed the quietest place on campus? Why did you feel the need to tell her my business . . . inaccurate business, at that?"

"Because she needed to know that you weren't, like, the average student, or whatever."

"Well, just so you know, I want people to see me as an average student." I tapped my foot impatiently.

"*You* want people to see you as average?" He pursed his lips as if I'd made a joke and he was the only one who got it, which wasn't entirely untrue. "Edie, I've known you for, like, a month, and I can already tell that you are not the type of girl who wants to be average. There isn't an average bone in your body." His cheeks pinkened as he spoke the last words.

"You're infuriating, you know that?" His small smile made me want to punch him in the gut and walk away, but it also made me want to grab him by the face and kiss him.

"Listen, I'm sorry I googled your disability. I'm sorry I said that to Makenna in the tutoring center." He pressed his hand to his forehead, his eyes on the ground. "I—"

I closed my eyes. My mom and Serena had both said that I wasn't giving him a chance. That his motives probably weren't malicious in any way, but this didn't feel right.

"Can we just forget we had this conversation and move forward?" Hudson asked, breaking the silence.

"No way," I said, trying to think of a good reason why I couldn't just let it go.

"No way to which, the forgetting or the moving forward?" he asked, taking a step toward me.

"Definitely the forgetting," I said as I pointed at him. My finger almost touching the tip of his nose. "We can move forward, but I'm not forgetting the fact that you googled me."

11

This Is Not a Riddle

I paced our room as Serena watched from her bed, eating Saltines with peanut butter.

"Just text him," she said, her mouth sticky with dry cracker and peanut butter.

"You're gross," I replied.

She stuck her cracker-covered tongue out at me. "If I'm so gross, then maybe you should leave, go meet Hudson in the quietest room on campus, and get tutored."

I stopped pacing to turn to her. My idea to solely rely on the FM transmitter and flash cards hadn't panned out. We took an in-class quiz I'd studied my ass off for, and I thought I did well, but turned out it was yet another fail.

"A couple days ago you were mad that he announced my business to the whole tutoring center. Now you're all *give him a chance?*"

"I wasn't mad; you were mad. If you remember correctly, I thought it was rude, but also thoughtful and adorable, and I'm not all *give him a chance*; I'm all *you need to pass French and your 'I'm going to do this myself' approach isn't working.*"

"You could help me study," I suggested, kicking at her dangling feet.

She nodded slowly as she chewed. "I can help you study, but I can't tutor you."

She was right. We stared at each other for a moment, her chewing slowly and me with my hands on my hips.

"Okay, I'll text him," I said reluctantly.

Serena clapped her hands twice with a smile. "That's the spirit."

I grabbed my phone from my desk.

> **ME:** Where is the quietest room on campus?

I hit send and held the phone in my hand, staring at my roommate as she dipped a finger into the peanut butter jar and then stuck it in her mouth. I shook my head as my phone vibrated.

> **HUDSON:** Is this a riddle? Like,
> what kind of umbrella do most
> people carry on a rainy day?

"See, this is exactly why this isn't going to work," I said, holding my phone out to Serena.

"What does it say?" She leaned forward, almost losing the sleeve of crackers that sat in her lap. She laughed as her eyes scanned what he'd written.

"Are you seriously laughing at this?" I pulled the phone back, my thumbs rested on the keyboard. I had no clue how to respond.

"I mean," she said with a shrug, "it is kinda funny."

I closed my eyes as I shook my head at both of them, even if only one of them was present to see it.

> **ME:** Are we meeting tonight for
> tutoring or not?
>
> **HUDSON:** Sure. The room is in
> the tutoring center. I can meet
> you there in 15 minutes.

"He can meet me in fifteen minutes," I said. "Happy now?"

"No, wait, what's the answer to his riddle?" Serena asked as she watched me drop my phone into my bag.

I raised my eyebrows to a record height.

"Come on, I need to know," she whined.

I sighed and pulled my phone from my bag.

> **ME:** My roommate needs to know
> the answer to your riddle or
> she will die.

I turned my phone so Serena could read what I wrote. It vibrated, and I turned it back to check.

"A wet one," I read.

"A wet one?" Serena repeated.

I shook my head again. None of this should have surprised me; Hudson was admittedly weird.

Serena laughed, and I looked over my shoulder at her. "What?"

"What kind of umbrella do most people carry on a rainy day?" She laughed again. "A wet one."

"Oh my God," I said as I finally understood the stupid riddle.

"A wet one," she said, laughing again.

I waved my hand, circling her direction. "You're out of control right now," I said.

"Tell him that was funny," she said.

"Absolutely not," I called as I closed the door, waiting until I was out of her sight to smile uncontrollably.

The quietest room on campus was pretty damn quiet . . . with the exception of Hudson's growling stomach and his tapping pen and his bouncing knee.

I had my notebooks, textbook, folders, flash cards, highlighters, pens, and pencils spread across the table. He had a fresh bag of Skittles, a pen, and his cell phone.

"Ohhh-kay," Hudson said, shifting uncomfortably in his chair as he took in all I'd brought. He sat directly across from me at the rectangular table that took up most of the stark white room. "We can start with grammar if you want." He bit at the skin around his thumb as he watched me drag my French notebook out from under the textbook.

"Grammar, okay. Sure," I said as I flipped through the lined pages. I'd recopied those notes three times. "Grammar." I opened the notebook to the page and presented it to him.

"How many times did you rewrite these?" he asked, his eyes wide.

"Three," I said, holding eye contact. One, because I wanted him to know that I was strictly business, and two because his eyes were just too nice to not look into. Which I guess negated the *strictly business* thing . . . but he didn't need to know that.

He exhaled. "Can I see your flash cards?"

I handed the stack to him and watched as he pulled off the rubber band. He flipped through them with one eyebrow raised and a quirk to the left side of his mouth. He tapped them back into a stack and thumbed the edges as he looked at me.

"Don't bend those," I said, watching his thumb strum down the edge repeatedly. He did it twice more. Completely ignoring me or to get under my skin? Either was possible.

The quietness of the room was putting me on edge. I thought it would be comforting to finally be someplace this quiet, but it was kind of unnerving. I took a deep breath in and out, my skin beginning to crawl.

"When you study these do you study French to English or English to French?" He held up a card that said *la nuit*.

"English to French, usually. Though I have tried it both ways. One doesn't seem better than the other," I said.

It didn't matter if I started with *la nuit* and translated to *night*, or started with *night* and translated to *la nuit*. On paper, I was doing okay. It was the out-loud part that I needed help with, and no real amount of memorization helped with that. The best I could hope for was enough word recognition to get the gist of a conversation and then guess at the rest. Which was similar to what I did most days, only in English.

"Okay, so for now let's go French to English. It's more important to work on vocab than pronunciation." He flipped through a few more flash cards, stopping on *l'avion*. "If we can work on you visually recognizing the words first, and understanding them when spoken second, you can pass his midterm and final. There are listening parts on both, but I think mathematically you could fail the listening sections but still pass with the writing and multiple-choice."

I nodded. But that wasn't really what I wanted. I did need to pass the course, but I also wanted to get some grasp of the sound of the language.

"Okay, French to English. Vocab. Recognizing words. Got it." I nodded, blowing out an overwhelmed breath. I tapped my thumbs against the table as Hudson flipped through my index cards again. "Except, I do need to practice the listening. I know you're just trying to help by saying that I could bomb the listening and still pass, which would be great if I wasn't spending the summer in Paris."

He stopped fiddling with the index cards. "When are you spending a summer in Paris?"

"This summer," I said, popping the top off my pen and clicking it back into place. "I leave June first, and I'm supposed to come back for the fall semester, but I'm going to opt to stay. Besides the graduation requirement, it's the reason I'm even taking French."

Hudson was quiet for a moment, his eyes on mine. "Well, that makes sense."

I watched his face as he spoke. He rubbed his forehead before setting the cards onto the table.

"What?" I asked. Clearly something was going through his head.

"Nothing." He shook his head, his eyes on the table. "This is really good work, Edie," he said, raising his eyes to meet mine. "I'm impressed."

I sat back in my chair, unsure of how to take his compliment and the change in his demeanor. "Yeah?" I asked, my voice squeaking.

"Yeah." He nodded, sitting back in his chair, mirroring me. We sat in near silence assessing each other, and it made me uncomfortable. The silence, not having his eyes on me.

"So now what?" I asked.

Hudson slid my notebook toward him. "I'm not sure," he said, flipping through the pages.

"What do you mean you're not sure?"

"I've never tutored before," he said, his eyes still on my notebook.

"You've never tutored before?" I repeated his words in a huff.

He shook his head before raising his eyes to meet mine. "I signed up to tutor for you."

"What?" I reached for my index cards.

"Yes," he said with a nod, freely handing over the stack. "You're my first toot-tee."

"Toot-tee?" I asked with a small laugh.

"Yeah, like I'm the tutor and you're the toot-tee."

I thumbed the edge of my index cards. "You're serious?"

"About the toot-tee thing, yes," he said, crossing his heart with his index finger.

I bit my bottom lip to keep from smiling. "No, I know you're serious about that." I crossed my arms. "Are you serious that you signed up to be a tutor just to help me?"

"Yeah, of course," he said with a shrug as he flipped through my notebook, thumbing to the last few pages. "Why is that so surprising?"

I opened my mouth to respond, but halted as he stopped on a page on which I'd sketched a figure.

He looked between me and the notebook, his cheeks turning pink. "Is this me?" he asked, the pink beginning to seep down his neck.

"No," I said too quickly, reaching to snatch the notebook, but not getting a finger on it before Hudson yanked it out of my reach.

It was him. There were two more like it if he turned to the next pages. Which I prayed he wouldn't—

"Wow." He moved to the next page, his eyes widening as his mouth dropped open.

"It's not you," I said with an indifferent shrug, reaching for the notebook again. Now my face was on fire. I couldn't have been less convincing if I tried.

His opened mouth turned into a giant smile at the next page. "You mean to tell me that these three sketches . . ." He turned the notebook so I could see the last figure. It was him in a navy fitted suit, a plaid button-down in purples and grays, and brown cap-toe oxfords. "Drawn in your French notebook, of a guy wearing a maroon hat—"

I pulled my lips in to keep from smiling.

"Aren't me? These three drawings?" He motioned to the page before. "That all look like me, all with brown hair and blue eyes, aren't me? That's what you're saying?"

I cursed myself for adding the maroon beanie. I brought my index finger to my mouth, my nail actually touching my teeth before I pulled it away. I was trying to hide my smile, but there was no avoiding it.

"Can I take these?" he asked, flipping between the three pages again. "I look good in these."

I nodded, silently agreeing that he could have them *and* that he looked good in them. I bit my bottom lip as he ripped the pages out one at a time.

He laid the pages in front of him on the table. "You're good at this," he said.

"Thanks." I felt like I could crawl under the table and stay there forever, but I appreciated the compliment.

His eyes scanned the pages again, then met mine. "What did the celery say to the veggie dip?"

"Huh?" I responded before giving myself time to process what he said.

He gathered the three pages and carefully stacked them. "I said, what did the celery say to the veggie dip?"

I shook my head with a laugh.

"I'm stalking you," he said, emptying one of my folders so he could slide the drawings in.

I bit the inside of my cheek. "Are you implying I'm stalking you?" I asked as he casually claimed my folder as his. I wasn't stalking him exactly, just observing.

"I am." He smiled, sitting down. "In pun form."

I opened my mouth to respond, but he interrupted me.

"Don't worry, I don't mind." He patted the closed folder. "At all."

12

Three Words: High-Fashion Lingerie

Friday nights were lab nights, and lab nights meant a minimum of two hours of sitting at a sewing machine, drafting patterns, or sketching out designs.

Tonight was a design night. It started as a sewing night, but then I stabbed myself three times in the same spot while pinning a zipper in place and quit.

The lab was a big space made small with all the equipment, boxes of fabric, and egos. There were also racks for clothes, mannequins for dressing, and rolls upon rolls of paper for drafting patterns.

I sat at a drafting table, the second one in on the right.

The row had eight tables, and for whatever reason I liked the second one from the window. Behind me was the main entrance to the lab; to the left of the door sat four rows of sewing machines. Five machines per row, twenty sewing machines. The sound of twenty sewing machines going at once was not a sound one chose to endure. At least it was a sound I chose to not endure. Hence the Friday night lab, a time slot no one else wanted.

Across from the sewing machines was a wall of floor-to-ceiling cabinets and industrial shelving, everything packed to the gills with fabric. Each box contained a different color, texture, weight, and weave. Distressed and fibrous. Lacy and plush. Silken and stone washed. Everything and anything you could imagine.

I was working on an assignment that had us each pick two terms—a style of clothing and a form of clothing—at random, and then design three pieces. My two terms were *intimate apparel* and *haute couture*.

Translation: high-fashion lingerie. I was going for boudoir meets Martha's Vineyard.

I'd been working on a two-piece brassiere and skirt for almost an hour, lost in my drawing and the soft music coming from my earbuds. The brassiere was two-toned, and the skirt was sheer from waist to midcalf, a thick opaque silk at the hemline. I pushed myself upright, my hands pressed into the table as I stretched my back. Hunching over the table could be murder on my back if I wasn't careful. I spun the picture to the left and then to the right, getting a look at it from both angles before reaching for my pencil.

I was happy with it, but it was missing something. It needed color, and my pencils were in my bag across the room. I pushed back from the drafting table only to be stopped almost immediately. I turned to look over my shoulder and screamed as my nose collided with a stomach.

I ripped out my earbuds and looked up at the same time, breathless.

"Jesus, how long have you been standing there?" I gasped, my hand on my chest.

"I don't know, like, five minutes maybe," Hudson said with a shrug, his hands shoved into his pockets.

"You've been standing over me for five minutes?" I wiped my forehead with the inside of my wrist, knowing I had pencil pretty much everywhere else.

"Probably," he said with a smile. "Actually, maybe longer."

I looked up at his smiling face. His rosy cheeks and piercing eyes.

"It's okay, I know what you're thinking and it's fine," he said, finally taking a step back.

"I don't think you have any idea what I'm thinking," I said slowly. The truth was I didn't even know what I was thinking. It was nearly midnight on a Friday night, and I was in a locked building. How the hell had he gotten in? How the hell did he even know where I was?

"Oh, well, never mind, then," he said as he pushed up onto his toes. Once, twice, three times.

"Did you want something?" I asked, the only question I could seem to get out. There were about a million running through my head, but that was what came out.

"I had something to tell you, and you weren't answering your phone."

My phone was across the room, in the same bag as my colored pencils. I hadn't touched it in hours.

"Who's celery stalking who now?" I asked as I looked up at him.

He looked back at me with a smile.

"Anytime now, Wes. What did you come over here for?" My stomach tightened. I didn't wish him around until he was standing in front of me. He was like the answer to a question I didn't know to ask.

"Oh, right." He bounced on his toes again once before rocking to his heels. "I came up with code names for us, you know, when we use the transmitter." He pointed to his ear.

"*Code names*? What does that mean?"

He laughed as he searched my face. I must have been wearing the thoughts running through my head all over my face. "Code names. Like names to call each other when we use the transmitter."

I shook my head, still not comprehending what he was trying to say.

"You know, like *the Eagle has landed* or *the Rainbow has left the sky*. You know, like that."

I nodded slowly as I watched his face. He loved that stupid transmitter. The first day he wore it he said it made him feel like a secret service agent and texted me about it the rest of the day. I neglected to tell him that I'd referred to it as the spy kit for years; I didn't want to give him the satisfaction of knowing I used to think it was cool, too.

"Oh-kay," I said, stretching out the word.

"What are you working on?" he asked, leaning over me. His heather charcoal jacket, the one with the stitched brand logo and perpetually popped collar that looked too good on him, brushed against my bare arm.

I held my breath.

"Who's gonna wear that?" he asked, turning his head toward me, his eyebrow quirked. His face was so close to mine I could feel his breath on my cheek.

"Probably no one," I whispered. Not because of the words, but because of the person hearing them. "It's just an assignment."

"You get to draw bras as homework?"

"Not exactly, but yes," I said.

"What else do you have?" He leaned over me again, reaching for a drawing I had already completed. "Please tell me you're going to make this one?"

I closed my eyes, knowing exactly what he was thinking as he tapped his finger against the sketch. It was a one-piece with layered silk at the hips and shoulders, but sheer everywhere else. Small cherry blossoms covered the groin, but only a sprinkling went up the bodice. It was delicate and revealing.

"I think Clément has this. Are you sure this is an original design?"

"Eww!" I said, scrunching my nose. "Some men can absolutely pull off lingerie, but him . . ." I shook my head as I pictured Clément in this particular article of clothing. Some things you just couldn't mentally unsee.

He smiled down at me. "You never know."

"Thanks for the imagery."

"Anytime."

"Well, I'm not making any of these. Sorry." I smiled as his face fell. He took one last look at the sketch before plopping into the chair at the next table. "Disappointed much?" I asked.

"That's a tragedy," he said, shaking his head, swiveling back and forth in the chair. "You're good at this," he added before pushing off and sending himself into a full twirl.

"So you've said."

"And I'll keep saying it," he said pointedly. "Because it's true."

I blushed, smiling at my sketches and then at him. "Didn't you have something you needed to tell me?"

"Oh, yeah!" He planted his feet and came to a halt facing me. "The nicknames. They're perfect."

I sighed loudly, exhaling as I slid down the chair and stretched my legs in front of me. I lifted my arms and folded them over my head. *This should be good.*

"So I was online, and I found a very scientific way to create a code name. I did yours for you." He smiled.

"How very generous of you . . ."

"Yours is Pink Peony," he said with a smug look. "Mine is Sergeant Style."

A burst of laughter came from somewhere deep inside me that I rarely tapped into. "How scientific could this system be if that is your nickname? Sergeant Style couldn't be further from an accurate name for you."

"Edie, it's a code name. It isn't supposed to be spot on. That's the whole point," he said as he pushed off the floor again and spun once.

"You seriously tried to get ahold of me for an hour about this, and then when you couldn't, you somehow celery stalked me to a locked building and then got *into* the building just to tell me this?"

Hudson's eyes lit up. He shook his head slowly as he watched me. "Edie," he said as he leaned into me, his face so close I felt his breath on my cheek again. "You have pencil on your forehead." He brought his thumb to his mouth and then rubbed it just above my left eyebrow.

I froze, my eyes closed briefly. "You did not just lick your thumb and then touch my face."

"I sure did," he said, sitting back and sending himself into another spin in the chair. "And I didn't celery stalk you; I happened to be in the building the other day and happened to walk by this room and then happened to see the sign-up sheet that said you were here on Friday nights. It's really all very innocent."

"Oh . . ." I don't know if *innocent* would be the word I would have used. "How very convenient that all those things happened to take place," I said, my eyes narrowing as I tried to hold in a smile. "But I don't believe for one second that you came all the way here, at this time of night, just to tell me about those code names."

I watched him spin in the chair, my insides twisting in all the best ways. It was obvious he just wanted to see me and as much as my insides loved it, my brain was repeating *Paris* over and over.

13

Your Enthusiasm Is Showing

"Okay, so I'm going to outer space tomorrow night. Want to meet me there?" Hudson asked as we walked across campus.

I'm going to outer space tomorrow night. Want to meet me there?

I nodded my head as I tried to process what he said, stalling.

"You have no clue what I just said, do you?" He nodded, mirroring me. He gave me a small shove with his shoulder.

"That obvious?" I shielded my eyes from the sun as I looked at him.

"Kinda." He was already picking up on my blank stares and delayed responses.

"What did you say?" I asked.

"Tell me what you heard first." He held open the door to the lecture building, ushering me in ahead of him.

The lobby was busy, and I had to squeeze in front of him so that we could stay together.

"I heard *I'm going to outer space tomorrow night. Want to meet me there?*" I smiled at the ground.

"That's exactly what I said. I booked us each a seat on the next mission to the Milky Way, and it leaves tomorrow night."

"Stop," I whined as I shoved him. "Tell me what you really said."

"I really said *I'm going to outer space tomorrow night. Want to meet me there?* Why don't you believe me?"

I clicked my tongue. "Whatever."

"What you thought I said is far more interesting than what I actually said."

"I don't doubt that." I held the door to the lecture room. "And for the record, we're already in the Milky Way . . ."

"What?" He scrunched his nose.

I laughed. "Earth is in the Milky Way; we could go to another part of the Milky Way if you wanted, but not the Milky Way itself. We're already here. It's like saying *let's go to campus* when we're standing in a building on campus. Campus is the Milky Way, Earth is this building."

"Say Milky Way again, please."

I shoved him lightly as we walked down the steps toward the front of the room. Hudson was teaching class today, which was great because ever since Dr. Clément nearly blew out my eardrum that first day, I was scared for my hearing every time he used it.

Hudson extended his hand, and I placed the transmitter in his palm. He slipped it over his head as he continued down the stairs to the front of the room.

"If you want . . . ," I started, hesitating as my stomach knotted. "My roommate has a volleyball game tonight, and I thought, if you were interested, you might want to go . . . with me."

"Yes," he said without missing a beat.

"You want to go?"

He smiled. "Yes, definitely."

I bit my bottom lip as my insides happily danced around. "I should probably warn you, I get a little . . . enthusiastic."

"There is nothing more I would want to do tonight than watch your enthusiasm," he said, taking a step away and toward the front of the room.

"Okay, eight o'clock in the big gym in Wyman Hall."

He hooked his thumbs onto the straps of his backpack and nodded as I slid into my seat.

I fished my notebook and pen out of my bag as people continued to wander in. Rustling papers and desks scuffing against the floor. Notebook pages fluttering open, binder rings snapping closed, pens tapping against desktops.

"Mic check one-two, Pink Peony." Hudson's voice was a whisper in my ear. "P.P."

I smiled at my bag, not wanting to look up at him.

"P.P., do you copy?" I shook my head as I pulled my notebook out of my bag. I didn't want to laugh and encourage his lame jokes. I'd already told him he was not to refer to me as *pee-pee*.

"Edie," he whispered.

I peeked up to see him smiling at me. I mouthed *hi*.

"Hi," he breathed into my ear.

I looked at my watch. It was a quarter to eight, and Hudson was nowhere in sight. I craned my neck to see around Terrance.

"Expecting someone?" Michael asked, his eyes on me as he drank his water.

"Yeah, your mom," I said before looking at my phone.

Michael shook his head, setting his water bottle on the bottom step of the bleachers. "One game?" he said walking backward onto the court. "Can't we just have one game of peace and quiet without the two of you making a scene?"

I bristled, but Terrance responded first. "We are the backbone of this team. You guys would be nothing without us."

I laughed as Michael rested his hands on his hips, staring

Terrance down. Terrance quirked his eyebrow, daring Michael to refute.

"Tell me we aren't the best part of this game," I said.

Michael shook his head.

"That's what I thought," I said.

Michael's eyes wandered toward the entrance. I followed his gaze and saw Hudson standing just inside the door.

"Hey," I said, breathier than I wanted as he walked over.

"Hey," Hudson said, his eyes on me. "That seat taken?" He gestured toward the open bench next to me.

"All yours," I said.

"Recruiting fans?" Serena asked. I hadn't seen her approach us.

"Yup," I said as Hudson settled into the seat next to me, though at a bit more of a distance than I would have liked.

"I love volleyball, you know?" Hudson said, his eyes on the court. "They say baseball is America's greatest pastime, but I think it's intramural volleyball. All the way."

I laughed.

"Who's your friend, Edie?" Terrance asked, speaking for my small crowd of friends that had gathered around.

"Hudson," he said with a kind of arching wave. "First-time attendee, longtime fan."

My eyes shot to Serena's, and she was already looking at me, her head listed. "So this is Hudson?" she asked, pursing her lips as her head bobbed, barely containing her smile.

"This is Hudson," he said before I could.

Serena's eyes landed on me again, her nose scrunched as she rested her hands on her hips. She opened her mouth to speak, but I interrupted.

"Oh, man, would you look at the time." I looked at my watch and then motioned toward the wall clock. "Game time." I clapped my hands together.

"Yeah, game time. Go on, get out there and win one for Daddy," Terrance said, shooing the players away.

"Eww," Miranda said as she took a few steps backward. "Don't ever say that again."

"Agreed," I said, looking at Terrance. I could feel Hudson's eyes on me, and it made my stomach somersault.

Terrance shot me a look before turning his attention to Hudson. He extended his hand over me, and Hudson took it. "Terrance Wyler, co–biggest fan of I'd Hit That, the best club volleyball team on campus."

"Wesley Hudson"—they shook hands—"primary biggest Edie Kits fan, the best—"

"Oh my God," I said, cutting off Hudson and burying my face in my hands. "This was a bad idea." I laughed.

Terrance grasped my shoulder, and I peeked at him enough to see a smile exploding on his face as he eyed me. "Is that right?" he asked, squeezing me.

"Absolutely," Hudson said, his voice serious. "Why, has the position been filled already?"

I laughed again, my face back in my hands.

"No, no, no." Terrance shook his head sternly. "That position has not been *filled* in quite some time." He squeezed my shoulder again.

"Edie's gone," I said, muffled through my hands. "She can't be around the two of you right now."

Hudson laughed. "But you invited me."

My head shot up as the referee blew the whistle to start the match.

"Yeah, you invited him, Edie," Terrance teased.

I shushed them both as Serena prepared to serve.

"Oh, damn," Terrance said, close to my ear. "Cody with the Cheekbones is gonna have a shit game tonight."

My eyes darted toward Cody. He was on the far side of the court, outside hitter. He was looking at me, his forehead wrinkled.

"Shit," I said.

"What's happening?" Hudson asked, leaning into me and Terrance.

I stiffened.

"Serena is about to score a point for our team," Terrance whispered, covering for me.

Hudson's eyes went to the court, but he stayed leaning into the conversation. "When will I know if she scores a—"

I was on my feet before the ref blew the whistle, Terrance

beside me. We bumped hips twice, elbows once, and then double high fives: our traditional first-point cheer.

"What was that?" Hudson asked, his eyes sparkling.

"That, my new friend, was the beginning of the end for the other team." Terrance crossed his arms with a flourish as he smugly returned his attention to the game.

Hudson looked at me. I could sense his smile without looking.

I shrugged, holding my shoulders up. "What? I told you I was enthusiastic."

"And I told you there was nothing more I wanted to see than your enthusiasm."

14

We'll Always Have Paris

I stood at a drafting table attempting to carefully rip a seam. I'd sewn it incorrectly, and now I had to rip it out and try again. Closing this side seam had been a serious pain in my butt.

"Michael's house is having a party tomorrow night," Serena said as a means of greeting as she took her position across the table from me. "Michael texted to see if you were going to actually attend one of his parties this semester."

"Did he?" I asked, looking up at her just as she snapped a picture.

"He did," she confirmed, leaning onto the table on her forearms. "He asked what you were up to."

"And what did you tell him? Because you know Friday is my lab night." I finished ripping out the seam and began picking the pieces of thread from the fabric.

She snapped two more pictures. "You can miss one Friday lab night—it won't kill you."

I shrugged. I could miss a lab night, but I didn't *want* to miss a lab night. Plus, I was so close to being done. All I had to do was finish the side seam I'd just ripped out and hem the bottom. One or two more Friday nights and it would be finished.

"How are you supposed to take pictures of me finishing this dress if you won't let me work on it?"

She snapped another set of pictures. "I've already gotten some good shots, and I'll get a ton more when you're finally able to wear it."

I sighed. Just thinking about finally getting to wear The Dress was amazing and terrifying at the same time.

"Is Cody going to be there?" I murmured. After the game the night before, despite how much fun it had been, I couldn't shake the feeling in the pit of my stomach.

"Yeah, maybe," Serena said knowingly. She shrugged once. "You didn't do anything wrong, Edie."

I knew I hadn't done anything wrong, but it felt like it. I liked Hudson, but I had rules. Cody had been playing by the rules all along, but when it came to Hudson, the rules were the last thing on my mind.

"Hudson told Terrance he was my biggest fan," I said, warming at the memory.

"It's pretty goddamn obvious he is." Serena snapped a picture.

I continued to pick at the cut threads.

"You like him, don't you?" Serena broke the silence.

"Paris," I said instinctually, though it hurt this time.

Serena huffed. "Forget Paris for five seconds. Do you like him?"

"*Forget* Paris? Seriously?"

"Do you like him, though?" she asked.

I cleared my throat. "No," I lied, lifting my head as I pushed the fabric to the side. "Only as a friend."

"Liar," Serena replied. "Admit you like him."

I crossed my arms. I would not admit that. Admitting that meant there could be a reason to keep me from going to Paris. Admitting that meant the possibility of regret. No. Edie Kits didn't do regret, at least not big-scale regret.

"I don't."

"You do," Serena said. "But I'll let you deny it."

"You'll let me deny it?" I asked with a chuckle. "Gee, thanks, boss."

She snapped a few more pictures.

"Can we talk about you for, like, two seconds?" I asked.

"I know what you're going to ask, and I don't want to jinx anything," she said, coming around the table so she was next to me.

I lifted the fabric, laying one piece on top of the other as I began to pin them together. These photographs were more than just an assignment; despite how Serena viewed her talent, they had the potential to win her a spot in the annual student art showcase. "I know there's a chance this project could win you some real attention," I said, ignoring her comment. "Do you think you have a chance?" I asked, rummaging through the pin box for all the yellow-tipped ones. "Like, am I enough to potentially win this for you?"

Serena set her camera on the table before adjusting her hoodie. She pulled at the cuffs, tucking her hands in, only her fingers poking out.

"Answer the question," I said. "Is this"—I waved over the pile of fabric that sat on the table in front of me—"going to make it?"

"I mean, maybe . . ." Serena pushed her hands out of her hoodie and into the front pocket. "I'd like to think that if I have the talent, then the subject doesn't matter." She tapped her left toe into the floor several times.

"And you do have the talent," I said.

She dropped her head back, her face toward the ceiling. "I don't know. A girl can hope, right?"

I laughed. "Someone with your talent doesn't need to hope."

"Boss," she said, righting her head. "I know you're all *woo-hoo, girl power* about what you do, but I'm not nearly as confident."

"I know you aren't," I said, putting down the chalk pencil I'd been holding. "But you are good at this. I would never bullshit you about that." I put my hands on her shoulders.

She let out a deep breath, her shoulders sinking a bit.

"Sewing machine." I gestured with my chin toward the bank of machines.

"I guess all I can say is that I'm going to try my hardest to make this project interesting and relatable," she said as she followed me to the sewing machine. "I feel like that's the most important aspect . . . that people can relate to it."

I adjusted the chair to my height and threaded the machine. "Absolutely," I said. "I'm just saying that I hope that this project is relatable."

She shrugged, pointing her camera in my direction. "I think everyone can relate to hard work and dedication to something they are passionate about."

15

Beer Pong? Beer Pong.

We walked through the living room at Michael's house, searching the crowd for his face, Serena's hand in mine as we made our way through all the people, our noses assaulted with the worst combination of men's body spray and stale beer.

"I don't see him," I shouted.

Serena responded, but I couldn't make out what she said. I looked over my shoulder so I could see her mouth.

"Kitchen," she repeated.

I nodded and pushed forward. The kitchen was in the back of the house, through the living room and dining room.

We passed two guys standing on the couch, sword fighting with plastic light sabers. A group huddled around the TV as two guys wearing headsets screamed and shot video guns with game controllers. We slipped past a couple whispering harshly at each other in the kitchen doorway.

"Not here, either," I said as I scanned the room, pushing onto my toes to see over all the heads.

Serena stepped up to a short, skinny guy with a shaved head standing in front of the refrigerator. Scott. One of Michael's frat brothers. "Where's Michael?"

"Last I saw he was in the backyard," Scott said, motioning toward the back door with his chin. He brought his beer to his lips and took a swig as he watched Serena.

"We'll be back," Serena said, running her fingers through her bangs. She grasped my hand and started to lead us through the kitchen and toward the back door.

"Hey, Serena," Scott called, his hands cupping his mouth. "Heads up, Michael is a gray barrette."

Michael is a gray barrette?

The backyard was far more crowded than the house, probably because it was fifty-five degrees out in March, which only encouraged people to hang out in the backyard like it was summer.

The backyard was small, surrounded on three sides by an old wooden fence teetering on dilapidated. Luckily for the neighbors on either side, who'd installed their own fences years ago, there was no chance of this backyard spilling into theirs.

"What did he say?" I asked Serena as we stepped outside.

"I have no idea. All I heard was *heads up*." She scanned the backyard. "There," she said, pointing toward a group of people standing around a set of feet in the air, cheering.

I pushed onto my toes again to see over the heads that separated us and whoever was doing a keg stand.

"Oh, shit," Serena said, sidestepping the guys standing in front of us.

The pair of feet in the air belonged to Michael. It was barely nine and he was already doing a keg stand.

"Gray barrette," I whispered to myself as I rolled my eyes.

"What?" She turned to me with an utterly confused look on her face.

"What I heard Scott say was *heads up, Michael is a gray barrette*; he was probably trying to tell you that Michael was doing something stupid in the backyard. People still do keg stands?"

"Gray barrette? That's what you heard?" Serena scrunched her nose with a giggle.

I nodded.

"Well, that gray barrette is going to make himself sick tonight," Serena said, shaking her head.

"Serena!" Michael shouted, his arms raised above his head, his hands in fists.

"Oh God," we both breathed simultaneously.

"Hey," Michael said once he'd jogged the few feet that separated us. "I'm glad you came." He completely ignored me as he ran a hand through his reddish hair.

I cleared my throat.

"Edie, my friend," Michael said, his attention finally turning to me. "You made it; so nice of you to grace us with your presence." His grin as lopsided as his stance.

I narrowed my eyes at Serena.

"Why are you always so dressed up?" Michael asked, switching gears quickly as he eyed me. His comment elicited a slap to the arm from Serena.

"Excuse me for wanting to look nice." I was way overdressed for this party, and I liked it that way. Skinny jeans, ivory camisole, navy blazer, brown riding boots. A plaid scarf in reds and blues to tie the whole outfit together.

I didn't dress up for anyone else; I did it for myself. I did it because I liked how it felt to be put together. Unlike Michael in his too-tight T-shirt boasting the symbol of a sports apparel company. Nothing like paying a company to advertise for them.

"I need a beer, STAT." I ran a hand through my hair, pushing it out of my face and tucking it behind my ear.

"Me too," Serena said as she assessed her date.

"There's something I have to do real quick. I'll meet you inside," Michael said, his arms outstretched, his fingers pointing in our direction as he walked backward toward the house.

"Shit," Serena said through a grimace.

"Ten bucks says the thing he needs to do is throw up," I said, my eyes wide. There was no way this would end well.

Michael's back was to the door when we walked into the kitchen. The room had mostly cleared out, the arguing couple nowhere in sight, and the guys stacking beer cans in the sink had left, too. Serena stepped up beside Michael, resting her hand between his shoulder blades as I stood behind him, smoothing my navy jacket and sniffing my scarf for any hints of stale beer.

"Hey," Michael said, wrapping an arm around Serena before turning to face me.

"Oh, look who it is," Serena laughed as the person Michael was talking to came into view.

"Hudson?" I said.

"Hey," Hudson said, shoving his hands into his pockets. He looked at me with that small smile that drove me wild. Not that he knew it drove me wild or anything, just that it literally put me back into the place where I either wanted to grab his face and kiss him or punch him in the gut, and right now I wasn't sure how I felt.

"Nice to see you again. Where's your hat?" Serena asked, pinching me in the tricep.

I could feel my face burst into flames. Kill me now. Someone. Anyone.

"Nice to see you again," Hudson said. "I forgot it." He looked at me. "The hat, that is."

The grin on Serena's face spread slowly as she looked between me and Hudson.

"Serena," I said through gritted teeth, shying away from another pinch to the underarm.

"What is going on right now? I thought it would be cool to invite Huds since he's such a fan of the team now. Right? Cool? Who cares if Hudson didn't wear his hat? Why don't either of you have a beer?" Michael asked, sincerely interested in the answer to every one of his questions.

"Huds?" Serena said, her eyebrow quirked.

"Beer pong?" I asked, changing the subject to something I knew would immediately distract Michael.

Michael reached into the refrigerator and grabbed four cans, handing them all to Hudson. "Beer pong," he said, grabbing out four more cans and handing those off to Serena.

The beer pong table was set up in the basement, and even though the basement had surprisingly high ceilings, high enough that Michael could stand up without hitting his head, it wasn't high enough for him to toss the pong ball the way he liked, which we knew. It gave us an advantage over them, though we were probably still going to lose miserably.

"Team names?" Michael suggested as he stacked his plastic cups in the traditional pyramid.

"Sure. Hudson, how about you think them up. I heard you're good at nicknames," Serena said, listing her head toward me.

I turned away from Hudson, shooting Serena the bug eyes.

"You heard about that?" he asked, pouring beer into each cup.

"I hear about everything," Serena said.

I gasped, swatting her in the arm with the back of my hand.

"There's an *everything* to hear about?" he asked.

"Oh, there's an *everything* all right," Michael said, grabbing everyone's attention. "And with these two, nothing is a secret."

A burst of air escaped me as I whipped around to face both boys.

"No, you didn't." Serena looked between Michael and Hudson.

Hudson blew out his cheeks, his face reddening by the second.

"What?" Michael asked. "You told me the other day in the campus center that Edie—"

"Oh my God, literally shut up right now." I laughed as I pressed my hands to my cheeks.

Hudson ran a hand through his hair. "How about Us versus Them?" he offered.

We all laughed at the pathetic attempt to change the subject.

"No." Serena shook her head as she smiled. "How about Ladies versus . . ." She held the word as she looked at me for help.

I stacked our cups. "Assholes?" I offered with a laugh, looking to Michael.

"Assholes works." She nodded enthusiastically, hip checking me away from the table. She wanted first toss.

"Oh, you're so funny, Edie. How could I have forgotten how funny you are?" Michael drawled. I playfully gave him the finger.

I watched Hudson as he continued to fill each cup with beer. He looked up at me when he finished, catching me watching him. "If it helps, I'm okay with whatever you've told Serena about me," he whispered, getting the attention of Michael and Serena as well.

I shot a look to Michael.

He shrugged with a smirk.

I blinked at him, my tongue skimming my bottom lip as I tried to conjure a worthy comeback for both of them.

"Can we just—" Hudson interrupted, gesturing over his shoulder with his thumb. "Like, over there for a sec?"

He stepped back from the table, his eyes on me.

I took a step toward him as I shot a look to my smiling roommate.

"Really?" I asked the second we were out of earshot.

He fidgeted with the cuffs of his shirt. "That guy has no chill."

"I have no chill right now, thanks to you," I said.

"Why, because you're so happy I'm here?" he asked with a smile as he took a sip of the beer he'd been pouring.

I shook my head in response, putting my hands on my hips. He gave away his smile so easily.

"You're really cute," he said, reaching for my arm and pulling me into him. "Come here." I was in his arms before I had a chance to protest.

"Impulse control issues much?" I laughed, my voice muffled by his shoulder, my hands still on my hips as he held me around the shoulders.

"Impulse control issues," he repeated softly, pulling me closer.

Hudson was hugging me. He was hugging me in front of people. Actually, he was squeezing me . . . a little too tightly. I laughed and tried to wiggle out of his hold. God, he smelled good.

"What the hell," Michael yelled from across the room. "Lady. Asshole. Can we play, please?"

16

Monsieur, S'il Vous Plaît

"**W**aiter, another drink, please?" I called to Michael, my arm stretched toward him as he stood over me and Serena. After our tragic loss at beer pong, we'd found our way to the love seat and hadn't moved since.

"I'm not being your waiter tonight. I already told you." He stood tall over us, his arms crossed.

"You've already gotten me, like, five beers. You are our waiter," I said, shooting him my cutest smile. Which, to be honest, probably looked pretty ridiculous. "And you don't want us getting drinks from strangers, do you?"

"She's right. We could get drugged or something. And

then how would you feel?" Serena said, draining her cup and lifting it toward him.

I turned my empty cup upside down. "You tell him, boss," I said, encouraging her. "Also, just as a pointer, you've been superslow with the drinks, so you might wanna—" I snapped my fingers repeatedly.

"Hear, hear!" Serena agreed.

Michael uncrossed his arms and then recrossed them. "Sometimes I really wonder how I put up with the two of you," he said.

"Oh, yeah? You won't be saying that to me in a few hours," Serena said, shooting Michael her best attempt at sultry in her current state, which included her awkwardly biting her bottom lip.

I covered my mouth, a laugh bubbling up as I watched Michael look at Serena. He was frozen, one cup in each hand. He had some decisions to make.

"Why a few hours?" He dropped our empty cups on the floor. "Why not now?"

"You're gonna have to be a little more convincing . . . ," she prodded playfully.

Michael left the room swiftly, returning with a tall, squared glass vase full of fake cream-and-light-pink dahlias. It was the kind that looked like it was filled with water, but it was squishy clear plastic, like something you'd see in the waiting room of a dentist's office. He presented the flowers with a dramatic flourish and a goofy grin.

I folded over onto myself, my nose to my knees as I laughed. The look on her face was priceless.

"Oh my God, stop it," she laughed, her hand over her mouth as Michael continued to stand there, arms stretched toward her, vase in hands.

I threw myself backward into the couch. I couldn't watch this. I was going to pee my pants if I kept laughing like this.

Serena extended her arm, and Michael hoisted her off the couch, tucking the vase under his free arm like a football.

"I can't," I said, trying to catch my breath. I held my stomach. Michael holding that vase full of fake flowers under his arm was entirely too much for me. How had that thing even gotten into their house to begin with?

"What'd I miss?" Hudson stepped into the small clearing around the couch. He looked at me, but I couldn't talk.

"*Nada*," Michael said, handing the vase to Hudson. "You watch this one." He pointed at me as he hooked his arm around Serena's shoulders.

"I don't understand this," Hudson said, spinning around the room looking for a place to set down the vase. He looked between me and the flowers he held with both hands.

"Which part?" I asked, finally curbing my laughter. "The vase itself or the fact that they even own something like that?"

"Both, I guess," he said. He set the vase on the coffee table across the room that had been pushed to the side to make space in the living room.

"Same," I said. "Sit?" I wiped away the tears of laughter from my eyes.

"Yeah, definitely." He smiled, plopping down next to me. His knee immediately started bouncing.

"That is gonna need to stop," I said, pointing to his leg and feeling like my movements were exaggerated by the alcohol.

"That doesn't stop," he said.

I watched him for a moment. His cheeks were rosy from the beer, and his hair was a mess from running his hands through it. I wanted to run my hands through it, just to see what it was like. This was only the second time I'd seen him without the beanie.

"Where's your hat?"

"I told you I forgot it." He touched his hair, confused.

"It's your most redeeming article of clothing. . . . Well, I guess it's more like an accessory."

"You noticed my redeeming accessory?"

"I mean, your sense of style is all over the place," I said, flicking at his blue-and-white-checkered button-down. "This has potential, but you have the sleeves rolled down like a nerd." I ran my finger over the cuff he'd been pulling at in the basement. It was evident that it was well fidgeted with over the years. The cuffs were worn and fraying in spots.

"Then roll them up," he said, offering me his arm.

I carefully unbuttoned the cuff, looking between his face and my fingers. He watched me closely. "Now pay attention, okay?" I grasped the cuff and pulled it up his arm to his elbow. "Pull the cuff all the way, okay? Don't start rolling it at the wrist."

He nodded as he watched intently.

I slipped my fingertips between the sleeve and his arm, the tops of my fingers brushing gently against his skin. "Then you fold this up to the bottom of the cuff." I smoothed the fold, adjusting and smoothing again once more before gesturing for his other arm.

"Do you want to try doing this one yourself?" I asked as I unbuttoned the other cuff. I'd been dreaming about dressing Hudson for weeks; this was the beginning of a dream come true.

He shook his head as he watched me. "You do it," he said, his face serious.

"Okay." I pulled the other cuff up to his elbow, then slipped my fingers between his arm and the shirt, taking a little longer than necessary.

"You know I'm going to Paris this summer, probably for the fall semester, too," I said as I tugged at a wrinkle in the cuff.

He let out a groan in response.

"What?" I asked with a laugh, giving his sleeve one last smoothing before settling back against the arm of the couch.

"You," he said as a means of explanation.

"What does that even mean?" I asked, my smile reflecting his.

"It means why are we talking about this?" he asked, dropping his head back against the couch, his face toward the ceiling. His knee started bouncing again.

"I was just saying," I said, shoving his shoulder. "Excuse me for caring about your feelings." I kicked at his bouncing knee.

He rolled his head my way. "You care about my feelings?" he asked with a megawatt grin I'd yet to see.

I blushed. "No!" I said, delivering a whack to his abdomen. He caught my arm and attempted to pull me into him.

"You care about my feelings, that's so sweet," he said, still trying to pull me.

"Let me go." I laughed as I tried to pull my arm back. He shook his head, tugging me a little harder.

"Let me go, Impulse Control Issues," I teased as I tugged harder. He let go and I fell back into the arm of the couch.

"You want impulse control issues? I'll show you impulse control issues." He fisted my scarf, kissing me hard.

I closed my eyes, feeling warmth spread through me as I kissed him. I'd been watching his lips for weeks in class, and now they were pressed to mine. They were everything I'd imagined. They were better than I'd imagined. My head swam.

The beer taking more control than I would have liked. But I was kissing Hudson.

I was kissing Hudson. Oh, *shit*.

I pulled away, putting my hand to his chest.

"No," I said, my other hand pressed to my forehead and then my lips.

He groaned in response, dropping his head back against the couch again. "That was a perfect moment, you know," he said as he rolled his head toward me. "I'd been waiting for the perfect moment, and that was it."

It was a perfect moment for eight months from then.

"You disagree?" he asked with a smirk.

He knew I didn't disagree. How could I dispute the fact that that had been an incredible kiss?

"So, you agree, then?" he continued when I didn't respond. "We just had a perfect first kiss." He smiled at me and opened his arms, inviting me into them. I stared at him and shook my head, unsure of what exactly he wanted. His arms were spread as he opened and closed his hands.

"Did you say first kiss? As in, you assume there will be a second kiss?" I asked, amused at the idea.

"Oh, there will be a second kiss," he said, his hands calling to me.

"I am not going to cuddle with you right now," I said. "And don't hold your breath on that second kiss."

He pouted, his arms still open. His hands still beckoning.

I released a deep breath. "Fine," I acquiesced, adjusting to lean on him, my cheek pressed to his chest.

He held his arms open until I'd settled, then wrapped them around me. It was an amazing sensation. The weight of his arms around me. The rise and fall of his chest as he breathed. He grasped my wrist and pulled my arm across his abdomen, releasing a happy moan as I settled my arm where he put it.

I closed my eyes. This was a bad idea, the best kind of bad idea, but still a bad idea. How long was I going to tell myself that I didn't like Hudson, especially now that it was clear he liked me?

"This is probably a bad idea," I said, adjusting into him.

"Nope. This is a great idea." He cupped my head against his chest; I could hear the smile in his voice.

I grinned, letting out a breathy laugh. "Can you get in trouble for this?" I asked. "The whole TA-student thing?"

He sighed deeply, his body relaxing into the couch. "We're a thing?"

I smiled as I shook my head. "No, *we* are not a thing," I said, tilting my head so I could see his face. "But the TA-student thing is definitely a thing."

"Then, no," he said, his eyes closed. His face calm. "But I'd be willing to get into all sorts of trouble over you."

"Ha. Ha," I said, resting my head against his chest again. His thumb grazed my ear and then my cheek.

"This is getting weird," I said, even though his touch was incredible.

"*Je sais. Ça va aller*," he whispered as his thumb grazed my cheek again.

If we stayed like this a moment longer, he would fall asleep. And I might, too. "I'm sitting up now," I said, half-heartedly trying to push off him.

He held me tighter. "Nooooo," he groaned.

"Yessss," I mimicked.

He squeezed me as he adjusted into the couch more, slouching and taking me with him. "Just five more minutes," he said.

I bit my bottom lip. I yawned as I settled into him. "Fine, five more minutes." I nuzzled my cheek into the softness of his shirt. "But that's it. No falling asleep, either." I poked him in the side playfully.

He shied away from another poke. "Sure thing, Edie." He breathed deeply, sleepily.

17

Eleven Sewing Machines Sewing

"So, you and Hudson, huh?" Serena asked as I climbed back into bed after a much-needed trip to the bathroom.

"It's too early for this conversation." I yawned, pulling the blankets over my head as I smiled to myself.

"Uh-huh, *sure*," she said, holding out the word playfully.

"It was nothing."

"It definitely wasn't nothing, Edie," she snorted.

"It was nothing," I said, laughing at her snort. "It can't be anything else."

There was a brief silence as Serena adjusted in her bed. "You really feel that way?" she asked.

I smiled at my blanket again. "No, not really."

"Did you just giggle?" she asked.

"No," I said, pressing my smile into my pillow.

"You are definitely giggling."

"Am not."

"You guys looked absolutely adorable cuddled up on the couch like that," she said. I could hear the smile in her voice. "You in that blazer and those ridiculous boots and him in the oldest flannel on the planet and dad jeans. I mean, honestly, how many plaid shirts can one person own? I bet he has dozens. Oh my God, I hope has an entire closet filled with them." I smiled at the thought of him.

"I'm a hundred percent sure he has an entire closet filled with them." I rolled onto my side. "Okay, subject change. You guys are up against Bump 'N Grind tomorrow night, and I really think you should have practice this afternoon."

"Are you serious right now?" Serena pushed herself to sitting.

I pushed myself to sitting as well. "Listen, when you beat them, you'll only have one more team to beat to go into the finals."

"Edie Helena Kits, shut up about volleyball," she said, tossing her pillow at me. "You are not changing the subject when you just admitted that you like Hudson."

I swatted it away, and it landed on the end of my bed. "Serena Elizabeth Theresa O'Dell, I said no such thing."

"He likes you," she said.

I rolled my eyes. "I have work to do in the lab today; do you want to paparazzi me or what?"

"Absolutely." She threw her blankets off and hopped out of bed. "But this conversation isn't over."

I followed suit. Throwing my blankets off and hopping out of bed. "You're right, there is plenty more to discuss about the game against Bump 'N Grind."

Eleven sewing machines chugged away as I attempted to concentrate on finishing up my fancy underwear project. I had my earbuds in, music blasting and Serena kneeling next to me taking "up-shots" of me working.

I was sharpening a lavender-colored pencil with my hand sharpener when my text message tone momentarily interrupted the music.

It was a text from Hudson. My heart jumped. My stomach flip-flopped. My smile exploded. I set the pencil and sharpener aside before opening the message.

HUDSON: Hey.

I smiled as I looked at the text.

Serena nudged me with her hip, mouthing Hudson's name. I nodded.

ME: Hey.

ME: Sorry about last night.

Still friends?

I picked up the lavender pencil when he didn't respond right away and began to sharpen it. Serena reached for my phone, tugging out one of my earbuds when she read what I'd written.

"Cold, boss," she said, setting my phone down hard.

"What?" I asked. I wasn't trying to be cold. I was trying to be pragmatic.

Serena pulled a chair behind me and hopped up. "Ten bucks says he isn't going to respond to that." She snapped a series of pictures from above.

"He'll respond," I said, twisting to look up at her. "He always responds."

"If you say so," she said as she hopped down. I watched her drag the chair back.

My stomach sank as I waited for a response.

I should text him again, tell him how much I like him. How funny I think he is, how awesome it would be to hang out and get to know each other better. How much I'd enjoyed his impulse-driven kiss . . . but then there was Paris. And sad good-byes. And regrets. And broken hearts. Texting him again would be a terrible idea.

I stared at my phone, waiting for a text from him. I shaded in the bustline of my sketch.

I checked my messages. I sharpened a jade-colored pencil. I shaded in some background. I stared at my phone again.

Why wasn't he texting me back? He'd been quick with the texts, and now, at the worst possible time, he wasn't going to answer me?

"Told you," Serena said.

I picked up my phone.

> **ME:** Are we still on for volleyball tonight?

"Why?" she asked, looking over my shoulder.

"Not helping," I said, dropping my phone facedown on the table.

My stomach turned. Why had I sent him that? I shouldn't have sent him that. That was probably the last thing he wanted me to text him.

I picked up a crimson-colored pencil and flipped to the next sketch as Serena continued to snap pictures and the music in my ears played uninterrupted.

18

Super Awkward, or Just, Like, Normal Awkward?

"Hey," Hudson said as he slipped into the desk next to me, rubbing his forehead.

"Hey," I said, not looking at him. I hadn't heard from him since I texted him, apologizing. Since I asked if we could still be friends. I'd watched the door at volleyball the entire game, even missing out on a few points. Three full days. Three full days I'd been left to wonder what the heck was going on in his head. Three days I ruminated over my words and his lack of response. And three days was a long damn time.

"That shouldn't have happened. I know you aren't—" He waved a hand around.

"Don't," I said, looking at him and then back to my earpiece. I'd been passing it between my hands as I waited my mandatory ten minutes. "Listen, I'm not looking for a boyfriend, or a friend with benefits, because everyone knows those arrangements always end badly. I need a tutor, and that's you."

He opened his mouth to speak, but I beat him to it.

"I'm sorry. I am. I like you and if this were eight months from now, then, trust me, we wouldn't be having any kind of conversation like this, ever. But it's not, and it is what it is."

"It's just—" He sighed loudly, before releasing a frustrated growl; my stomach tightened in response.

"I really like you." He blurted the words as if they would burn his mouth if he didn't, his eyes shooting to the front of the classroom and then back. "And I don't believe in bad timing."

I lifted my head from my hand as the sounds of the room increased. "Can we just be cool?" I asked, knowing those were the wrong words the moment they were out of my mouth. "I mean, can we just, you know, rewind?"

"*Bonjour, tout le monde!*" Dr. Clément said as he approached the podium and slipped the transmitter over his neck. Shuffling papers and scraping chairs took my attention away from Hudson briefly.

He opened his mouth to respond, but he said nothing as he pushed out of the desk. *Later?* he mouthed as he took a step backward.

I nodded as I slipped on my earpiece.

"Okay, it's awkward," I said to Serena as I slid into the chair opposite her in the dining hall.

"How so?" she asked as she chewed her bagel. Today she expanded her culinary horizons to include buttered noodles; a huge pile sat on a small plate next to the other half of her bagel.

"I hadn't heard from him since I sent him that text, and then he plopped down next to me before class and I said that it shouldn't have happened, and then he said he *really* likes me." I picked up my sandwich with the intent to take a bite.

"How is that awkward?" she asked sarcastically.

"Because obviously, I am an asshole," I said, deciding against the bite.

"Well," she said, "yes and no."

"Tell me the yes." I crumpled up the napkin I was holding, tossing it to the side and crossing my arms.

"You are kind of leading him on," she said with a bite of noodles. "But, like, I mean that in a purely girls-can-do-whatever-they-want-with-a-guy-and-just-walk-away type of way. You don't owe him anything, per se, but he's a great guy so I kind of feel bad for him, you know?"

I shrugged as I picked a piece of lettuce out of my sandwich and tossed it aside. "And no?"

"Well, you told him you didn't want anything, right? Like, he knows about Paris."

I looked just over Serena's shoulder and out the windows that made up the back wall of the dining hall. It gave a perfect view of the lake across campus.

"You didn't tell him, did you?"

"I did tell him, but it came out all shitty."

"Well, don't you think you should tell him in a nicer, less shitty way?" she asked, crossing her arms and leaning back in her chair. "Or else we're going to have another Cody on our hands."

I shook my head, deciding to take a bite of my sandwich, chewing as I thought it through.

I swallowed the mouthful of food. "Part of me doesn't want to tell him anything more than I already have," I said. "The other part of me knows better."

"The part of you that doesn't want to tell him anything more is the part of you that likes him, so that makes sense."

I ran my fingers through my hair. "I told him I just needed a tutor," I said with a grimace. "Like, I actually said I didn't want a relationship, I just needed a tutor."

"If you weren't my best friend, I would call you an asshole."

I pushed my tray aside and rested my head in my arms. "Call me one anyway."

"Nah," Serena said as she rummaged through her bag. "That would let you off too easy. You need to talk to him and make this right."

"And how am I supposed to do that?" I asked, lifting my head from my arms just as she snapped a picture of my miserable face. "Noooo," I whined, putting my face back into my arms.

The camera clicked a few more times before Serena rummaged through her bag again, putting her camera away.

"Just talk to him. Tell him what's up. Be honest." She laughed. "You know, just like you always tell me to be with Michael."

"Yeah, and how does it go with Michael?" I asked, my nose pressed to the table.

When Serena didn't respond, I said, "Besides, honesty didn't work with Cody." I sat up, my hunger outweighing my need to sulk.

"That's because you never liked Cody this much." Serena snagged a chip off my tray and popped it into her mouth.

"And you don't think it's the same situation with Hudson?" I said, swatting her hand away from taking a second chip.

"You don't think he likes me more than I like him? Like, on a scale of one to ten, he's at an eleven and I'm just not."

"Edie," she said, her chin sinking to her chest as her eyes stayed on me. "Don't be ridiculous. You might not be at an eleven, but I haven't seen you like this in a long time. You don't both have to be at an eleven, and you know that, so stop asking me if it's the same and start asking yourself."

19

Do You Like Me? Circle Yes or No.

"**W**hat aren't you telling me?" Hudson asked the moment he stepped into the quiet room. "I know something's wrong. Please just tell me."

My head shot up; I'd been looking at my phone as I waited for him. "Huh?"

"You like me, but—" He threw his arms wide. "You're sorry about what happened at Michael's party? There's nothing to be sorry about. I'm not sorry I kissed you." He smiled, his eyes shining in the bright lights of the room.

I shushed him. "Close the door."

I narrowed my eyes at him as he shut the door. I barely dragged myself to this tutoring session, considering the way we'd left it at the beginning of class, but my conversation with Serena had turned me around enough to come. I had a whole speech planned, which was out the window now.

"So, what did you mean by that?" he asked, breaking the serious amount of silence the room provided. "Are you really sorry you kissed me back?"

My heart raced. I took a deep breath in through my nose and blew it out my mouth. The room was unnerving.

"I am sorry. If I led you on in anyway, I'm sorry for that."

He scoffed as he put his hands on his hips. "You aren't leading me on, Edie." He shook his head, his eyes settling on the wall to the left. He shook his head as if he was talking himself out of saying something.

"Can we just agree that this is all we are?" I asked, motioning between the two of us.

Hudson shrugged. "Yeah, sure," he said, his eyes finding mine.

"That was not a reassuring *yeah, sure.*"

"I'm good, okay? *Promettre.*" He took the seat across from me.

"Promise," I translated.

"But can you at least admit that if I had texted you the same things you texted me after the party, you would have questions?"

I rested my head in my hand, my eyes still on his. "Maybe I would. Probably not, though. I don't know."

"*Menteuse!*" he said with an annoyed laugh.

"Fine, maybe I would be a little interested," I acquiesced. "But only because I'd be wondering why you even bothered to text me such a nothing statement."

"Then why did you text me such a *nothing* statement?" he asked, finally deciding to sit in the chair across from me.

"I don't know. Because I'm an idiot." I threw my hands up, letting them drop onto my thighs. This was not going the way I had planned it to go in my head. I was supposed to tell him I was sorry and that we needed to remain friends until I came back from Paris . . . if he even wanted me when I came back.

"You're not an idiot," Hudson said, leaning on his elbows, his fingers reaching for me across the table.

I pulled back just as his fingertips skimmed my forearm. "Don't defend me to myself."

He considered me for a moment, his hand still frozen in the spot I'd jerked away from. His head fell forward for a moment before he pulled himself upright. "Fine," he said, motioning for me to hand him my notebook. "Let's just get started."

He flipped through the first few pages, stopping at the beginning of *chapitre trois*. His thumb tapped the notebook. I could hear his knee bouncing under the table.

"What?" I asked. The air in the room had changed. It was heavy and hard to breathe.

He shook his head as he spoke. "Nothing." His eyes still on the notebook.

"*Je suis désolée*," I said not knowing why, only knowing that something had changed.

He took off his hat and ran his hand through his hair a few times before pulling it back on. "It's okay, you don't have to apologize." His eyes were on his hands now as his fingers twisted together.

"Clearly I do," I said, my eyes frozen on him. He watched his fingers as I watched him. The silence of the room settling in on us, surrounding us, closing in on me.

The room was getting to me. I began to breathe through my nose—out through my mouth, deep calming breaths. The silence was too heavy, too foreign a feeling. I shut my eyes, willing away the sense that the room was literally closing in on me.

Hudson's eyes moved from his hands to my face as I leaned my elbows on the table and rested my face in my hands.

"What's wrong?" he asked, sitting up and pushing away from the table. "You okay?"

I nodded, my eyes closed, my face toward the table. I breathed deeply. In through my nose and out through my mouth, panic quickly rising inside me. "This room—"

"You're not okay," he said, coming around to my side

of the table. He squatted next to me, his hand on my shoulder.

I breathed deeply once more. In through my nose and out through my mouth.

"Talk to me," he said, his hand moving from my shoulder to my back.

This had happened to me only once before, during a physics lesson on sound waves where we all took turns wearing noise-canceling headphones. We were each supposed to wear them for about five minutes. I'd lasted less than a minute. The silence too foreign, too uncomfortable. The last time we'd been in this room we talked the entire time, so despite the unease, I had been able to sit through it.

His touch sent goose bumps down my arms. "It's too quiet in here." I breathed out the words before taking another deep breath through my nose. "I can't be in here."

"Let's go, then," he said, standing abruptly and pulling at my arm. "Get up, we're leaving."

I let him tug my arm, but I didn't move.

"Come on." He dropped my arm and started collecting my things. "There are other places we can study. Wherever you want is fine. Or the library. We can go to Clément's office or the student center. We can go anywhere, Edie. Want to go to the lab? Your fashion class lab? We can go there—"

He was rambling. His suggestions stringing together into one long word as he stuffed my things into my tote bag. He hiked it onto his shoulder before attempting to lift me out of the chair by my armpit.

"Hudson, stop," I said, not pulling away but stiffening. "I can stand up on my own."

"Okay. All right. I'm sorry. I just thought I would help if you needed it. You know, if you were unsteady or something. I just—"

I pushed off the table and stood, my eyes finding his and halting his rambling. I pressed my hand to his chest and he instinctively placed his over mine.

"I'm okay," I said, squeezing my eyes closed. "This room is just making me feel claustrophobic or something."

"I'm sorry. I shouldn't have stopped talking. I should have known it would be too quiet or that you might get upset."

"How could you have possibly known that?" I asked, pressing my fingertips softly into his chest, wanting him to stop rambling. His hand pressed harder into mine and mine into him. I could feel his heartbeat against my palm. I closed my eyes as it pulsed. I could hear it; he was the one that needed to calm down. "Just give me a second."

"Okay, yeah, right," he said, pressing my hand to his chest.

"Thanks," I whispered, my eyes still closed.

"*En français*," he whispered back. I could hear the smile in his voice.

"*Merci*," I said, a smile pushing at the corners of my mouth.

"*De rien*." He breathed out deeply.

"You're welcome," I translated.

"I think you're going to be just fine." He squeezed my hand again.

I nodded, letting the heat from his chest spread through me, the warmth of his touch pulling me into him. I took a step toward him, opening my eyes into his.

His eyes searched mine, flicking back and forth between them rapidly.

"Are you going to be just fine?" he asked nervously.

I nodded. "Yeah, I think so." I took another step toward him, pressing my body into our joined hands.

He released my hand, moving his to the nape of my neck. His other hand cupped my face.

I wasn't sure what was happening, but I knew I wanted it. It felt right. This moment. This feeling right here and right now.

"*J'aimerais t'embrasser*," I whispered, my eyes locked on his.

He shook his head, his eyes pleading with me silently.

"No." I took a step back and out of his grasp, wrapping my arms around my middle. "You're right."

He shook his head again, his arms still floating as if I were in them. "I—" he started, dropping his arms.

The silence settled around us once again, but this time I wasn't going to let it get to me. This time I was going to run.

20

That Hoodie Life

"Stop lying to yourself, Edie. You messed up and now you regret it," Serena said as she paced the room gathering textbooks.

I wasn't lying to myself; I knew I messed up, and of course I regretted it. I hated regret.

"You look like total crap, too, FYI," she added. She stopped in front of me as I sat on my bed.

I sighed as I rested my chin in my hands and strummed my fingers against my face.

"We've lived together for a year and a half now, and I've

seen you in sweatpants and a hoodie more this weekend than ever. It's unsettling, if I'm being honest," she said with a fake shiver.

"Ha ha." I looked down at my crossed legs. I had been wearing the same heather gray sweatpants since Friday. I picked at them as Serena continued.

"Seriously, Edie," she said, pulling at my arm to get me to look at her. "I've never seen you this mopey."

I looked up, chin still in my hands. Serena wasn't wrong, I was mopey, but I couldn't get anything done because I couldn't concentrate on anything but Hudson. The interaction we'd had in the quiet room.

"I can't see you like this," she said, turning on her heels. "Your hair is a mess. You're wearing zero makeup, and I've already mentioned your clothes."

I had so much work to do. I'd gotten a few things done, but I couldn't even look at my French book without feeling like total crap.

"I can't deal with this level of miserable," she added.

She couldn't deal with my miserable? It wasn't like I was handling my miserable any better.

"Just call him, please." She turned back toward me. "Or text him. Or email him. Or send a carrier pigeon. Or, like, I will go to his room and personally hand him a note. Just do something with yourself."

I let my head fall back as I stared at the ceiling.

"Plus, we have a game tomorrow night and we need you," she said.

"I'll be there," I said, righting my head only to catch Serena with the camera aimed my way. "Don't you dare!" I said, putting my hands up to shield my face, but I wasn't quick enough.

"I need to document your misery," she said, capping the camera. "For a different project. I'm going to call it 'A Girl on the Brink of a Life of Solitude: The Edie Kits Story.'"

"I hate you," I said, flopping onto my side.

"You don't hate me. You love me." She hiked her tote bag onto her shoulder. "And we need I'd Hit That Superfan Edie with the Style present and accounted for at our game tomorrow night. Don't let us down, boss."

I sighed. "I'll be there, don't worry," I said. Serena threw me a smile over her shoulder as she left the room.

I looked at my phone as the scene from the quiet room played again in my head. Me telling him that I wanted to kiss him and then him telling me no . . . but then the way he held my face. How sweet his eyes had been.

ME: I'm sorry.

I stared at the words. Send or don't send? Send or don't send?

I pressed send and put it into the universe's hands.

The phone vibrated against the bed almost immediately.

> **HUDSON:** I should be the one
> apologizing.

>> **ME:** No. I'm the one who said
>> I wanted to keep things strictly
>> in the friend zone, but then I
>> tried to kiss you in what felt
>> like another perfect moment.

I smiled as I remembered his argument for our first kiss being the perfect kiss.

>> **ME:** I don't blame you for
>> telling me no and letting me
>> walk away.

I dropped the phone before I could send anything else.

It vibrated once, twice, three times. I stared as it lay face-down on my yellow quilt.

> **HUDSON:** It felt perfect to me too.
> **HUDSON:** Which was why I said no.
> **HUDSON:** I can't have another
> perfect kiss with you only to have

you wake up the next day and
realize it was all a mistake.

Oh . . .
The phone vibrated again.

> **HUDSON:** I could punch myself
> in the face for letting you walk
> away unkissed. I don't know what
> I was thinking.
> **HUDSON:** I keep reliving it in my
> head over and over.
> **HUDSON:** I guess I'm a glutton
> for punishment.
> **HUDSON:** Like I said, I would
> get into all sorts of trouble over
> you.

I couldn't help but smile. I dropped the phone and sank my face into my pillow, hiding the blush that crept down my neck. I pressed my smile into the pillow before pulling away and picking up my phone.

> **ME:** So you wanted to kiss me?
> Despite all the stupid things I said.

The phone vibrated before I had a chance to set it down. I smiled before I even opened it.

HUDSON: Yes.

      ME: Despite knowing how I feel?

HUDSON: Yes.

There was no way out of this. It would be so easy to fall for Hudson, hook, line, and sinker. It would be so easy to be with him, be happy . . . but that only led to pain. A pain I didn't want to feel, let alone put him through.

      ME: Knowing that I leave for Paris on
      June 1 and might not return until the
      spring semester?

I hit send knowing exactly how he would respond.

HUDSON: Yes.

I pressed my palm into one cheek and then the other. They were starting to hurt from smiling.

      ME: SMH.

I expected the phone to vibrate immediately, but it didn't. I opened the text box and then closed it. Opened it and closed it again as I waited. Maybe he didn't know what else to say. Maybe he felt like he'd said too much—

The phone vibrated before I could finish my thought.

> **HUDSON:** Can I see you tonight?
>
> **HUDSON:** I need to see you tonight.
>
> **HUDSON:** Will you meet me in outer space? (aka my dorm room)

I smiled as I texted him back.

> **ME:** Yes to both.

21

The Many Talents of Wesley H.

I checked Hudson's text again to make sure I was at the right place before I knocked on the heavy door covered with magazine cutouts of superheroes and villains. Two name tags adorned the top, obviously made by the RA on the first day. WESLEY H. and his roommate, STEPHEN J., but Hudson's WESLEY was covered by a picture of a chocolate chip cookie ice cream sandwich, because of course it was, and his last name had been handwritten in marker. There was a picture of puppies in a wheelbarrow below that, along with another of a hamster eating a tiny doughnut. The most interesting was a picture of a half-naked girl holding an Xbox controller.

"What's this?" I asked when Hudson opened the door, my finger on the picture of the half-naked girl. In fairness, it was closer to Stephen J.'s side of the door so it probably wasn't an addition made by Ice Cream Sandwich H., but still.

"That's Trisha," he said without missing a beat. He stepped out of the doorway, ushering me inside. "She's working her way through law school."

"Aren't all strippers?" I shot back.

"Actually, they prefer the term *exotic dancers*," he said, rocking onto his toes.

"So how did Trisha, Xbox enthusiast and exotic dancer working her way through law school, end up in a magazine that was then taped on your door?" I said, shifting my weight as my stomach fluttered. I was in Hudson's room. We were talking about something totally stupid, but I was there and he was there.

"Now, that's a great story," he said, taking a step toward me.

"I'm sure it is," I said, watching him. He took another step toward me until we were nearly chest to chest. His eyes were heavy, like he'd been meaning to sleep for days but just hadn't gotten the chance.

His room was cleaner than I expected. It was cleaner than most college guys' rooms. His side of the room was sparse. His desk was spotless; a laptop sat closed in the middle with only a pen to keep it company.

The only thing on his wall was a giant whiteboard calendar/corkboard, each block filled in with an event, but on the corkboard side, displayed for the world to see, were my three sketches pinned evenly, one next to the other. Well, maybe not the world, but at least anyone who walked into this room.

"You seem to be just full of good stories, Wesley Hudson," I said, batting my eyes at him teasingly.

"I really am. It's just one of my many talents," he said with a yawn as he ran a hand through his hair.

"Is that right?"

"Yeah, I've got loads of them." He brought his thumb to his mouth, biting at the skin around his nail.

"Stories or talents?" I asked, pulling my bottom lip through my teeth. I wanted to kiss him so bad it hurt.

"Definitely both," he said, breathy, his eyes on my mouth.

I closed the gap between us as I spoke. "Prove it." I looked up at him, fisting his shirt like he'd done to my scarf at the party.

"Shit," he whispered as my lips pressed into his. He pushed his hand into my hair, cupping the back of my head, and I melted into him.

I pulled him closer, one hand holding his shirt and the other snaking up his chest and around his neck.

"We can't," he said against my lips, his breath hot on my mouth.

"We can." I nodded as he took a step away, his shirt pulling out of my hand. My fingers instinctively moving to my lips.

He breathed out deeply, his eyes on the floor as he shook his head. He looked up at me before moving to his bed, patting the spot next to him. "I want to, trust me, I really want to." He pressed his eyes closed tightly, resting his head against the wall.

"But you can't because I ruined it," I said, deflating.

He patted the spot next to him again, and this time I moved. I climbed onto his bed and sat next to him, our backs pressed into the wall.

He slid his hand across the bed and into mine. "I'm sorry."

I closed my eyes and leaned my head against the wall, too. "Where's your roommate? Where's Stephen J.?" I asked, trying not to focus on all the mixed signals I was giving off.

"Stephen J. is not here."

"Clearly," I said with a laugh.

"I kicked him out like twenty minutes ago and told him to get lost," he said with another yawn. "I told him that you were coming over and that I wanted to be alone with you."

I turned toward him slightly, my left shoulder against the

wall. "For how long?" I asked. I brushed his hair off his forehead, my fingertips grazing his face.

Finally. I'd been waiting so long to do that.

"How long do I want to be alone with you?"

I nodded.

"Forever, of course."

"I really want to kiss you right now, but that was the corniest thing you could have said." I searched his face as his eyes closed and another yawn escaped.

"Being corny is one of my many talents," he said.

"I'd love to see more of your"—I cleared my throat—"talents, but after that joke, I don't know, you might be too corny for me." I brought his hand to my mouth, pressing my lips into his knuckles.

He closed his eyes and shook his head. "No. I can't have this back-and-forth. Either we can touch each other or we can't. You're saying no, but you're acting yes."

I dropped his hand, my face turning into a frown. "I'm sorry."

"Don't be sorry, just be honest." He pulled my hand into his lap. "Because I don't want this whole will-they-won't-they thing. The whole *we can't be together because I'm leaving and blah, blah, blah*. Either you're in or you're out."

I sighed.

"Listen, this isn't do or die. How much trouble could we

get into? Let's just do what feels right and figure it out later. . . ."

"But still . . . ," I said with no intention of finishing the thought.

"But still what? You want to keep it strictly business. I don't like that, but fine. We can keep it strictly business. I just can't have it both ways." He shook his head, his eyes drifting to his lap, his voice faltering slightly. "I can't do it."

When I didn't respond right away, he looked up at me. My eyes were already on him, searching for the right answer.

"Can you just kiss me, and we'll overanalyze it later?" he asked, his words so soft that I would have missed them had I not been looking at his face.

I bit the inside of my cheek. "I can," I whispered as I leaned into him. He held my face in both hands, his thumb grazing my bottom lip as he moved closer.

"So, how do you like outer space?" he asked, his breath hot on my face. "It's nice this time of year, right?"

"It's perfect this time of year," I whispered as my lips brushed his.

"Perfect for second *and* third kisses?" he asked, pressing his lips to my jawline.

"Don't get ahead of yourself." I smiled against his lips. "But, yes, to both."

22

It's Called Science, Duh

ME: Can we study for the quiz?

I was in the lab on a Saturday, which was not a Friday night, and I was feeling overwhelmed for more than one reason. It felt instinctual to text Hudson. We didn't need to study, but I wanted to see him.

I set my phone down as I continued to pin the pleats of the bubble skirt I was working on. Beautiful deep purple with a wide waistband made of a cotton blend. It was the perfect summer day skirt, not too billowing, but full and bouncy.

I checked my phone again. Nothing.

> **ME:** I'm about to take your silence as
> a "yes, of course we can study" if you
> don't text me back in 5 seconds.
> **ME:** 4
> **ME:** 3
> **ME:** 2

My phone vibrated in my hand. I smiled as I saw his name pop up.

> **HUDSON:** Sorry. Migraine. Out
> of commission.

Oh. Oops.

> **ME:** Is there anything I can do
> to help?

I cringed as I hit send. I didn't want to text him again—obviously he was not feeling well—but I couldn't just let him suffer alone.

I held my phone as I waited for a response, quickly researching migraines. All I knew was what my mother used to do.

My phone vibrated.

HUDSON: I hear migraines don't
exist in outer space.
HUDSON: Book me a flight on
the next trip.

The following items were accompanying me to Hudson's dorm room: one gel eye mask, one nighttime eye mask, one break-and-shake ice pack, one heating pad, two bananas, one Pepsi and one Coke, three bottles of water, peppermint-scented face cream, a dozen or so glow-in-the-dark stars, and my lavender-scented pillow.

I hesitated as I stood at his door, the strange collection of pictures staring me down. I took a deep breath and then knocked lightly.

I pushed onto my toes and rocked back on my heels as I waited. No answer. I knocked again, a little harder this time. I brought my index finger to my mouth, my nail touching my teeth, wanting so badly to bite it.

Nothing.

I knocked again one last time; if he didn't respond, I would leave.

"Hudson," I whispered through the heavy door as best I could. "It's me, Edie."

I heard a muffled rustling, a sneeze, a painful groan, and then the click of the door unlocking. Hudson squinted at me through a crack in the door.

"I, um." I stumbled over my words. He looked awful. "I'm here to help." I grasped the strap of my shoulder bag, motioning to it with my chin, trying to convey my bag of, hopefully, helpful remedies.

He closed his eyes, his right hand coming to his temples as he rubbed them both, thumb and index finger. He nodded before stepping away from the door and into the room.

I waited a second, one brief moment where I wondered if I really should have come over. If anything I brought would even help.

A groan came from in the room. "Are you coming?" Hudson moaned as the springs on his bed squeaked.

I stepped into the room, squeezing through the crack of the door, trying to keep the hall lights from spilling into his room. I shut it behind me, my back pressed to the door as I hesitated.

"I looked up some stuff about migraines, and I brought a few things that might help," I whispered, or I spoke in as close to a whisper as I could. I moved farther into the room, only the glow from his laptop's power cord and his roommate's alarm clock lighting my way. "Can I help?" I asked as I stood at the head of his bed.

"You can try," he said.

"You might have to move around a little," I said as I began to unpack my tote. "Is that okay?"

He sighed deeply, punctuating it with a groan. He was lying on his back, his fingers pressed into his eyes and his face in a grimace. He was in sweatpants and a beat-up hoodie with a football team logo across the chest.

"I'm going to need you to take your hoodie off," I said, grabbing the peppermint lotion. I'd read that the smell of peppermint can ease a migraine, and when I called my mom for advice, she said she used to rub it onto her chest, like vapor rub for congestion.

"Edie," Hudson breathed, his fingers working in a circular motion on his eyes. "My head is literally killing me right now, but if you want me to remove my hoodie so that we can make out, I will." A hint of a smile perked his left cheek.

I rolled my eyes at him even though I knew he couldn't see me. He moved slowly. I reached to help him sit up, but he was seated before I could. He dragged off his hoodie, holding it out to me but dropping it to the floor before I could catch it.

"Okay, lie back down but keep your head off the pillow," I said as I waited for him to move. I slid the tube-shaped pillow between his neck and the bed. "Is that comfortable?"

He adjusted it before confirming. "Smells like you," he murmured.

"It's actually lavender-scented. I use it when I'm stressed out, but, like, I heard it works for migraines, too," I said.

He brought his fingers to his eyes again. "It's definitely Edie scented," he said.

"Here," I said. "Lift your head one more time." I stretched the nighttime eye mask as he lifted his head. I slipped it over his eyes, carefully releasing the elastic in hopes that the pressure wouldn't make the pain any worse.

He adjusted the eye mask against his face. "Please tell me these aren't feathers I'm feeling," he said with a smile as he pulled lightly at the mask. His hair was everywhere, sticking out around the elastic band in some places and flattened in others.

They *were* feathers. Bright pink and yellow feathers to be exact, along with the word DIVA written across the mask in rhinestones.

"Nope, no feathers. Don't know what you're talking about."

"Okay, fine." He rested his hands at his sides. "What's next?"

The next step was the peppermint lotion, but rubbing it on his chest . . .

"I'm, um, I'm gonna rub something on your chest . . . ," I said. "Is that . . . would that be okay?"

Hudson lifted his T-shirt without a word.

I warmed the lotion in my hands before lightly pressing my fingers into his collarbone.

He hummed softly as I rubbed it in.

"It's peppermint. My mom said it helps."

"This is really weird, but also kinda kinky," he said. "The face mask, the lotion . . . Please, please tell me you have some handcuffs in that bag," he added drily, though I could hear the smile in his voice.

"Wesley Hudson, if you weren't in so much pain already, I would hurt you."

He laughed again, strained as I rubbed the last bit of lotion into his skin. I pulled his shirt back down as I spoke. "Okay, so I have to turn the light on, but just keep that mask on and it won't let any light in," I said, taking a step back from the bed.

"I almost don't want to know what's coming next."

I shushed him as I flipped the switch near the door. His room was a wreck. Clothes everywhere. His notebooks spread across his desk as if dumped in a hurry. His backpack sat upside down with the contents spilling out. It was the opposite of the last time I'd been here.

I bent down to pick up his bag, shoving papers and a folder back into it as I lifted it onto his desk chair. A packet of papers sat on his closed laptop; several sentences were highlighted in bright yellow and a blue Post-it sat just under the highlighted section.

"In a case in which a Teaching Assistant has a personal relationship with a student (i.e., family relation, romantic, friendship, etc.), it is advised that the Teaching Assistant disclose the relationship to the overseeing professor. Based on the role of the Teaching Assistant, the professor has the authority to make a decision regarding the ethics of said relationship."

The Post-it had a few words scribbled on it in quotes: *"I don't care what you do, Hudson. The French are not a people who will stand in the way of love."* I smiled at the note. He must have spoken to Clément. Why was I not surprised that Clément didn't care one bit . . . or that he was the type of guy who would speak for an entire country of people?

I set the paper down, my stomach tightening as I peeked at Hudson before getting to work on the next step of my plan.

"Almost done?" he asked after a minute of quiet.

I looked over at him as I affixed the last plastic star to the wall. He was still on his back, the lavender pillow under his neck, the DIVA face mask covering his eyes. He looked kind of ridiculous, but he also looked like he was feeling better. His voice sounded better, at least.

I didn't say anything as I walked across the room, running a finger up his bare arm as I passed him. He pulled it away out of instinct, laughing and rubbing it with his other hand. "Goose bumps," he whined.

I flipped the switch, returning the room to its original

darkness except for the glow-in-the-dark stars. I smiled at them. At Hudson lying unaware. At how good it felt to be with him.

"I'm going to replace this mask with a different one, okay? But just keep your eyes closed." I leaned over him as I slipped off the DIVA mask, my hair running lightly across his face. Before I could set it aside, his hand slipped into my hair, cupping my head.

I pressed a hand to his chest. "Let me put the other mask on you, okay?"

He massaged his fingertips into my scalp. "Quickly."

I slipped the gel mask over his head, adjusting it over his nose and around his eyes. "Is that okay?"

"Does this one have feathers?" he asked, touching it with the hand that had been holding my head.

"Nope, none," I whispered. I pressed my hand to his chest again as I pushed to stand.

He wrapped his hand around my upper arm, pulling me back to him. "Lie with me," he whispered, his eyes still closed. He scrunched his forehead, releasing a pained breath.

"I have some other things for you, like I brought some water and a couple sodas for the caffeine. . . . I wasn't sure if you liked Coke or Pepsi, so I brought both, and—"

His hand moved from my arm to the back of my head, pulling me into a kiss.

"But—" I said against his lips as I tried to pull away,

wanting to kiss him, but also wanting to finish my treatment plan.

"Edie," he said, his lips still against mine. "Just lie down with me."

I kissed him once before carefully climbing over him, lying on my side between him and the wall; his arm was out-stretched for me. Once I settled he wrapped it around me, pulling me in. I rested my cheek on his chest, breathing in the lavender and peppermint. Breathing him in as well.

"You can open your eyes," I said, looking at the stars on the wall at our feet.

"I don't want to," he said with a small grunt. "It hurts to open them."

I sighed. I should have known better. Oh, well, he'd see the stars another time.

"Outer space," he whispered.

I lifted my chin to see that he'd lifted his mask.

"You did this?" he asked.

"Did what?" I asked. I pressed my lips to his jawline.

"You put the stars up?" He rested his palm against my cheek, holding my head to his chest.

"Don't be ridiculous, we're in outer space. I didn't put the stars in the sky. Don't you know anything about sci-ence?" I teased.

"So then what would science call this particular constellation?" he asked, slowly lifting his other arm, waving to the wall of stars.

The stars were arranged in a giant high heel shoe. The points angled to convey a stiletto. It was a pretty damn good depiction, if I did say so myself.

"La Stiletto, named for the Greek goddess of fashion, obviously." I waved my hand toward the wall as well.

"Look at you, mixing French and Italian like a pro," he said with a laugh and then a pained cough.

I tilted my head to look at him. "Are you feeling any better?" I asked. "Like, on a scale of one to exploding head?"

He moved ever so slightly to look into my eyes. "On a scale of one to exploding head I'm at a six," he said with a wince as he kissed my forehead. "What did the orange say to the juice box?"

I opened my mouth to respond, but closed it.

"I can't concentrate when you're around," he said with another laugh and pained cough.

"You need to stop laughing," I said, pursing my lips to contain a smile. "Especially at your own jokes." I poked him lightly in the side.

"But laughter is the best medicine," he said, shying away from another poke.

23

Sometimes I Just Like to Smile at My Notebook, NBD

"**Y**ou look really pretty today."

I looked up at Hudson, shaking my head. My cheeks were on fire, and I didn't even try to hide it. Class hadn't started yet, and he was already abusing the transmitter.

"You do."

I looked at him with wide eyes. These weren't walkie-talkies, so I couldn't talk back. He looked really good today, too. I raised an eyebrow as I looked him up and down, making sure he knew I was checking him out.

I looked him up and down again.

His laugh came through, and I smiled in response.

"Keep that up and I'll announce to the whole class how pretty I think you look today," he whispered, his back to the room as he wrote on the whiteboard. *Adjectives*. "And maybe I'll tell them about our trips to outer space."

I pressed my lips together as I smiled at my notebook. The room was beginning to fill, and with the heat on full blast I was dying with my hair down. I hesitated, fumbling with the hair tie I kept on my key ring. I didn't want to put my hair up; one, because it wasn't part of the look I was going for today and two, because of my earpiece.

I closed my eyes, willing myself to just do it. To just put my hair up and not care if people saw the earpiece. Why was I so concerned about what other people would think? Why did I care so much? Almost twenty years old and I was still the thirteen-year-old afraid to let anyone see me.

Screw it. It had to go up.

"Hey."

I looked up as I pulled my hair into a low ponytail. Our eyes locked.

"You look great."

I watched as he wrote on the board. *Content. Drôle. Beau. Talentueux. Doué. Mignonne.*

Happy. Funny. Beautiful. Talented. Gifted. Cute.

My eyes were trained on his every movement. Now I couldn't look away if I wanted to. Screw the earpiece; just having Hudson as a teacher was helping me focus more than any assistive technology had.

"Stop looking at my butt," his words came through in a whisper, his back still to the room.

A burst of laughter escaped, loud and obvious. I slapped my hand over my mouth, eyeing the people around me who stiffened at my outburst. The girl in front of me even turned around. I mouthed *sorry* to her with a shrug, and when I looked up, Hudson was looking at me with that smirk that made me question whether to kiss him or kill him.

"You need to stop," I said, my hand open, waiting for my transmitter.

It was the end of class. I stood near the back of the room waiting for everyone to leave and for him to pack up. The rest of the lecture had gone on without any more outbursts, thankfully, but I could still feel the heat in my cheeks.

"I didn't do anything," he said, feigning innocence. He slid his hand into mine instead of handing over the receiver.

"Not in class," I whispered, pulling away from him.

"No one is here," he said as he stretched his arms wide.

I opened my hand to him again, and this time he set the device in it.

"You're abusing this privilege," I scolded.

"I can't help it. It's just too perfect," he said as we walked.

"I can say whatever I want to you—get you to laugh out loud—and there's nothing you can do about it."

"Yeah, and that's no fair." I casually linked my arm through his once we stepped out of the building.

"But it's such a beautiful thing to see your face turn pink as you smile at your notebook," he said, shoving me playfully. "And that laugh, oh my God, I could never get sick of your laugh. That was too perfect. You have to admit that was so perfect."

I tried my hardest to hold in a smile to match his. "You enjoy torturing me, don't you?"

"I really do," he said, pulling me into a side hug. "Speaking of torturing you . . ." He pulled his backpack off one shoulder and spun it around his body.

"Speaking of torturing me?" I asked, eyeing him as people passed us in a rush to their next class. I watched as he dug around in his bag.

"I got you something," he said as his hand stilled in his bag. "Close your eyes."

"I'm not closing my eyes," I said. I crossed my arms, jutting out my hip.

"Close your eyes, Edie," he warned, squinting at me.

I sighed deeply, rolling my eyes at him before closing them.

"Keep them shut," he said. "I mean it."

"Okay, okay, I—" I started, but stopped as I felt Hudson

pull a hat onto my head. My hands immediately went to the hat to pull it off, knowing it was going to ruin my hair more than I already had by pulling it into a ponytail.

"Don't you dare take that off," he said, his hands over mine.

I dropped my hands slowly in surrender. "Can I open my eyes now?"

"Yeah," he said.

I opened my eyes to see Hudson's phone in selfie mode, his smiling face watching my reaction. "I got you one, too," he said as I looked at myself on the screen.

I touched the beanie as I pulled my bottom lip through my teeth to keep my face from splitting in two. He'd gotten me his exact beanie but in a soft pink, close enough to rose quartz to make me wonder if he'd actually listened to me ramble on about the color at the volleyball game.

"You like it?" he asked, bouncing on his toes, the phone moving with him.

I looked from him to my own face and then back. I pulled at my hair, adjusting my ponytail to lie over my left shoulder. I checked the phone once more before pushing his hand out of the way and pulling him into me.

"This is adorable," I whispered, my lips touching his neck as I spoke. "Thank you."

"You're welcome," he said. "Let's go back to your room and hang out."

"Can't," I said with a pout as I released him. "You know I have Media Econ."

"After?" he asked.

I touched the hat again, touched my hair. "You mean when you have German Lit?"

He shrugged his backpack strap onto his shoulder. "I don't need that class," he said, reaching for my hand.

I shook my head. "No, I'll see you tonight for *tutoring*. We need to study for the midterm," I said, watching the smile spread across his face.

"Sure, we can study for the midterm." He let go of my hand as we backed away in different directions. "But listen, I think we should study in your room, or mine, doesn't matter."

I put a hand on my hip and listed my head. "Nice try."

"No, really," he said, taking a step toward me. "I did some research about quiet rooms, and did you know that Microsoft has the quietest room on earth? It's in *Guinness World Records*. And people have had hallucinations and stuff. Felt panicky just like you did."

"Oh-kay," I said calmly, though my pulse was starting to race just thinking about being in that quiet room again.

"What I'm saying is, let's be proactive in avoiding hallucinations of any kind and steer clear of the quiet room. Which leaves my room or your room as the next best thing." He reached forward and touched my hair, twisting my ponytail around his finger twice.

I looked at him, searching his face for any sign of teasing. "You're serious?"

"Yeah, totally. I guess the longest anyone has ever stayed in this room was forty-five minutes. People couldn't stand to be in there, literally—if you are going to go inside, you have to sit. For whatever reason it really throws off people's equilibrium, too."

"Okay," I said after a moment. "We can study in my room . . ." I grasped his hand, pulling it away from my hair before dropping it. A big smile spread across his face. "After your German Lit class!"

"Sure, after class," he said, taking a step backward.

"I mean it!" I said.

He took another step away, his thumbs hooked on the straps of his backpack. "I know you do," he called, still walking backward. "But studying *you* is way more important than German Lit will ever be." He raised his arms over his head.

"Oh my God, stop it!" I said, hiding my face in my hands. We were standing in one of the busiest places on campus, between two of the busiest class times. If my makeup wasn't perfect, I would have pulled the hat down over my face.

"Not a chance!" he said, arms still in the air as he turned and walked toward his next class.

24

It's How I Know You're . . . Uh . . . Awesome

"So for every correct flash card, I'll take off an article of clothing," Hudson said as we sat at opposite ends of my bed, needing as much space between us as possible.

"No deal." I shook my head. He was right, studying in my room was way more relaxing than the quiet room had ever been. It was a good idea, but suggesting he remove an article of clothing for every correct answer? That was a terrible idea that would end with little to no studying.

"Okay, so then I'll just take my clothes off now." He moved to pull his shirt over his head.

"Stop, Hudson, I seriously need to study," I whined.

He dropped the hem of his shirt with a pout, but pulled his beanie off instead. He ran a hand through his hair, ruffling it.

"Less pouting, more helping."

"Less helping, more kissing?" he suggested.

"Some tutor you are," I said, throwing a pillow at him. "Good thing I'm your only toot-tee; I'd feel bad for anyone else who had to endure this kind of treatment just to learn something."

"Come here so I can learn you a thing or two." He opened his arms to me like he had when we were on the couch at the party.

"About French?" I asked.

"Yes, definitely about French."

I groaned as I flopped onto my back. "I'm gonna fail this midterm, and it's going to be all your fault."

"Awww," he said as he crawled over everything scattered across my bed. He propped himself up over me on his forearms, his hands on either side of my head, holding my face. "You aren't going to fail the midterm."

"I am, though." I covered my face with both hands.

"You know way more than you are giving yourself credit for, you know that, right?" He nosed at my hands.

I pulled my hands from my face. "I really don't, though."

"That's better," he said as he looked into my eyes.

"Wes?"

"Yes?" He hummed as he ran his thumb over my bottom lip. His eyes on my mouth.

"If you don't get off me and help me study like a good TA, you are never, ever touching my Ts or A again."

"Well, now that certainly is something." He listed his head as he brushed my hair away from my face and behind my ear.

"It certainly is."

"Can we talk about the whole 'figuring things out later' thing?" I asked. Every minute I spent with Hudson I felt like I was slipping further and further into the relationship zone.

Hudson shifted, rolling onto his side, his back pressed into the wall. "Sure," he said, folding my pillow in half under his head. "It's all figured out."

"Oh-kay . . . ," I said, holding out the word. "Do you mind elaborating on that?"

He skimmed his thumb against my forehead, smoothing out the lines. "Can we just agree to keep things as they are at the moment?"

"And how are *things* at the moment?"

"This. Us."

I nodded. Us. "Okay."

"Okay?" He smiled.

I nodded again. "Want to meet me at the shop on Friday? I can show you what I've been working on."

"I'm going home on Friday," he said.

"You're going to be gone for a whole weekend?"

"I'll be back on Sunday."

"But—"

"It'll be all right." He lifted his arm, and I scooted into him. "And then you can show me all the things you've ever worked on."

I laughed. "Be careful what you wish for." I traced the letters on his shirt with my fingertip: I'M NOT YELLING, I'M GERMAN. "And thanks for caring."

"*Pas de problème!*"

"No problem," I translated as I continued to trace the letters.

"*Je vais te manquer ce week-end?*" he asked.

"*Te manquer. Te manquer.*" I repeated the word I didn't know, my eyes on his shirt. I got the *I will* and *weekend*, but not the rest. "*C'est quoi, 'te manquer'?*" I asked, looking up at him.

Hudson's chest moved as he laughed lightly.

"*C'est quoi, 'te manquer'?*" he repeated. "*Tu vas me manquer* is how I feel every time we're apart. . . ." He paused for a moment.

I bit at my bottom lip as I waited for him to continue trying to decode his words, pulling from all the French I could remember.

"It's how I know you're . . . awesome."

"Awww, you think I'm awesome?" I asked, poking him in the side. "Thank you so, so much."

He pushed himself to sitting to avoid another poke, retreating to the end of the bed.

"It's true, I do think you're awesome," he said with a shrug.

I sat up, pulling my knees to my chest. "Oh, well, then, tell me more," I teased.

He pulled a small stack of index cards from his bag and waved them at me. "First, I made these especially for you."

"Special index cards? That's so . . . *awesome* of you." I put my arms up to protect myself from a pillow sailing toward my head. "You're so *awesome* at throwing pillows. I can't wait to see these *awesome* new flash cards."

"*Génial,*" Hudson said, tapping the stack of index cards against his palm. "Awesome."

"*Génial,*" I repeated. "Great, now you can tell me how awesome I am in two languages."

He pointed the index cards at me, an eyebrow quirked as a smirk played across his lips. He cleared his throat as he sat up straight, tapping the stack against his palm again. I sat up straight, mirroring him.

He held up the first card. *Avant-garde.*

I clapped my hands, dropping my knees and crossing my legs. I leaned my elbows onto my thighs. "*Avant-garde*: when one introduces an unusual idea or something experimental in fashion or the arts."

"*Très bien*." He flipped to the next card. *Boutique*.

I listed my head with a sigh. "A shop or store." That was an easy one.

Chartreuse.

"A shade of green. Yellowish green." I scrunched my nose. "Not a favorite of mine."

Minaudière.

"An adorable clutch," I said, watching Hudson's eyebrow quirk. "A clutch, you know, like a little handbag you would bring to a fancy party."

He smiled and flipped to the next card. *Ombré*.

"Oh my God," I sighed as I shook my head. "When one color fades into another."

"What?" he asked, turning the card to face him.

"Ombré is just so overdone right now. Everything is ombré. Or chevron. If the next card says chevron, I'm leaving," I warned.

"This is your room." He laughed.

"So?" I said as he flipped to the next card.

Une jupe.

I squinted at the card as if looking at it harder might help. I didn't know it. I shrugged. "Can you say it out loud?"

"*Une jupe*," he said with enunciation.

I shook my head.

"Skirt," he said, flipping to the next. *Les talons aiguilles.* I shook my head again.

"High heels," he said. "A stiletto heel." He ran a hand through his hair, his cheeks turning pink.

"Like the famous constellation La Stiletto?" I said.

"Exactly." He smiled down at his crossed legs before flipping to the next card.

Les vêtements.

"Clothing!" I laughed, glad to finally know one.

"Okay, last one." He ran a hand through his hair again, his cheeks deepening to red.

I squinted at him. "I don't like the look on your face right now."

He flipped the final card. *Ménage à trois.*

"You're an ass," I said, lofting the pillow back at his head.

He lifted his arms to protect his face, his laugh muffled. I threw another pillow at him, then a stuffed animal.

"Okay, okay! Sorry!" I stopped throwing things at him as he slowly lowered his arms. "I just wanted you to be prepared when you're in Paris. If I know French men, they'll definitely be asking—"

"Oh my God, Hudson!" I yelled as a purple stuffed elephant hit him in the face.

25

That's What We Call a Win-Win-Win-Win Situation

Clément's office gave me the same sinking feeling in my stomach as it had the day I first set foot in there, the day I reached out for help and had my hand slapped away. Now I waited for him to tell me that I failed the midterm. That I would need a ninety-nine or something on the final to pass, which would never mathematically happen. It didn't help that the girl who'd been in his office before me left crying, either.

I wore my new beanie. I felt safe in it. I felt more like myself in it. It was the perfect pick for me. I had no idea how he pulled that off, but he had. I needed the courage to face

Clément, and the beanie gave me that because I wanted to scream at him. I wanted to tell him that this was his fault. That I wouldn't have failed the midterm had he just allowed me the few accommodations I needed from the beginning.

"You passed," Dr. Clément said, interrupting my quickly mounting doubt. "But only just."

"Excuse me?" I asked, briefly wondering if I should have said *excusez-moi* instead.

"You passed," he repeated, slowly and louder.

Okay, well, that was fair. He probably thought I didn't understand him.

"You earned a seventy-two on the midterm. You hold a sixty-six in the class," he said, turning my test toward me as it lay on his desk. "And if you get at least a sixty-five on the final, you will pass the course."

"Wow," I said, reaching for the corrected exam. A seventy-two wasn't *only just passing* in my opinion. A seventy-two was awesome! A seventy-two was amazing! A seventy-two was . . . not a grade I thought I would ever celebrate, but still!

"Can I keep this?" I asked.

"No." He took the test from my hands. "I do not allow students to retain their tests."

"It would be a really good study tool for me and—"

"No," he repeated. "But if you would like to look at it, you may do so during office hours."

"Oh, so I can come in and look it over, I just can't bring it home?"

He slid my test back into an overfilled file folder. "*Oui.*"

"Okay, great. Well, thank you for letting me know," I said, beginning to gather my things, cursing myself for assuming the worst. My hard work was paying off.

"Wait, this is only half the reason I asked for this meeting," he said, waving me to sit back down. "I wanted you to know that I believe you are working as hard as you can. I believe you want to pass and that this is, indeed, very difficult for you."

Whoa. Dr. Clément acknowledging my hard work? Was there a hidden camera in here somewhere? Besides the few teachers in high school who really knew me, I only ever heard that from my mom.

"*Merci*," I breathed.

"I passed the midterm, and Clément said I could look at my test when I'm with you," I said, rushing through my words as I slid into the chair across from Hudson. "Well, actually, he said I could see the test during office hours, but whatever."

Hudson was in the library for his normal two-hours-every-Monday-Wednesday study session in which he would have his books open, notebooks out, but spend the entire time talking to the people around him . . . whether he knew them or not.

"Tell me something I don't know." He leaned back in his chair, linking his hands behind his head.

I eyed him. "You knew I passed and didn't tell me? *Très impoli.*" I reached into my bag and pulled out my notebook and flash cards. "So rude."

"*Très bien,*" he said, his eyes smiling. "When did you learn that phrase?"

"A while ago," I said with a smug one-shoulder shrug. "Figured I would need to use it against you at some point."

He beamed at me, shaking his head slowly.

"You're wearing your beanie," he said, tapping his pen against the notebook that sat untouched, but opened, in front of him.

"Clearly. Don't change the subject," I warned, pointing a finger in his direction. Trying to stay serious around him was impossible.

"It looks good on you."

I huffed, crossing my arms over my chest as I leaned back in the chair. I raised an eyebrow at him.

"Okay, sorry for not telling you that you passed the mid-term," he said with a sigh, only saying the words because he had to, despite the way he looked at me.

"So, give me my test right now to make up for your

rudeness," I said, diffusing all the butterflies in my stomach from the gleam in his eyes.

"I don't have it." He released his chair and clunked forward, his elbows landing softly on the table.

"What? Why not? You knew we would be studying together at some point." I gestured at him with my stack of index cards.

"Whoa, calm down," he said, a smile creeping across his face. He was laughing at me. It made me want to punch him. It also made me want to kiss him.

"I will jot down what you need to study based off the midterm, and we will study from that, okay?"

"I mean, yeah, I guess that would work, but I still would want to see my test, you know, just to see what exactly I did wrong and—"

"You wanna go on a date?" he asked.

I paused. "A date, as in, do something other than snuggle, and study sometimes?" I feigned surprise.

He clasped his hands together behind his head again. "Yup."

"With you?" I asked.

"No, with that guy." He unclasped his hands to motion toward a scraggly haired older man sitting two tables away.

I smiled as I flipped through my flash cards again. "You're an idiot."

"An idiot who you'll go on a third date with?"

"Third date? When did we even have a first date?" I argued, listing my head as I ran my fingers through my hair.

"The volleyball game," he said, "was date number one, and the party was date number two."

"First of all, the volleyball game was not a date, I was just being nice," I said, trying to brush off the fact that it probably . . . definitely . . . could have been a date. "And second, Scott and Michael's party was a party."

"No." He smiled, listing his head to match mine. "I knew you would be there, *and* I asked you to meet me there. I mean, you thought I was asking you to meet me in outer space, but really, I was asking you to meet me at Scott and Michael's. Plus, I asked Michael to ask Serena to ask you if you were coming just to make sure."

I pressed my fingertips to my mouth as a slow smile spread across my face. Okay, well, that explained a hell of a lot of things. "You knew I had no clue what you said that day, though."

"Right, but does it matter anymore?"

I ran my tongue across my bottom lip, trying to think of a comeback.

"So yeah, third date," he said when I didn't respond.

I flipped my hair over my shoulder. "*Touché*."

"Bravo!" he responded. "So, will you go on a date with me?"

I shook my head slowly, my eyes glued to his. "Maybe,"

I said as I thumbed the edge of my stack of index cards again. "Just get me that midterm, and then we'll talk."

His smile crept slowly. "I get you the test, and you'll go on a date with me?"

"*Peut-être*." I shrugged, playing indifferent.

His eyebrow quirked. "Can I pick the date?"

"No, I already have something in mind." I twisted the rubber band around my index cards and then dropped them with a light thud onto my textbook.

"Wait, you were already thinking of asking *me* on a date?" He grabbed my index cards and thumbed the edges like I had just done.

I shrugged. "Yeah, kind of."

"You were going to ask me on an already-planned date whether I got you the midterm or not?" He continued to thumb the index cards as he watched my mouth.

"*Oui*." I nodded. "But now I get the midterm, too, so it's a win-win for me."

"And I get a date with you?" he asked.

"Of course." I snatched the index cards from his hands before he bent the edges.

"Well, then, that's a win-win for me, too."

26

Who Are You and What Have You Done with Hudson?

The lobby of the college's performing arts building was buzzing. The doors had opened minutes earlier, but there was no rush to get inside. I stood off to the side, contemplating leaning against the wall as I wiggled my toes in my heels to get the feeling back.

I checked my phone—no messages, other than the eight panicked messages from Terrance about his crew not being on time for the show that was about to start. Hudson was already ten minutes late—not for the show, but I'd asked him to meet at seven, when the doors opened. Where was he?

"He here yet?" Serena asked as she approached, Michael in tow.

I put my hands on my hips, listing my head at her.

"Right," Serena said, shoving me playfully. She knew I was annoyed. "Why don't we go and get our seats, and we'll see you in there, okay?"

"Yeah, that's fine." I huffed, letting myself deflate a little.

"You look good, though," Serena said, using a finger to size me up and down as she took a backward step.

I smiled. "Thank you." I grasped the hem of my olive green chunky-knit cardigan and fell into a small curtsy. "See you in there," I called as I pulled at my hair. I scanned the room, fidgeting with the end of my braid; I'd twisted the front down and into a loose side braid. I turned back to the doors, one hand on my hip and the other playing with my hair, my shoulders rolled forward, when I saw him. He'd been standing there watching me.

"Hi," I breathed as I took him in. He looked absolutely perfect. Navy fitted chinos, a maroon-and-navy-plaid button-down, and a gray blazer, just the top button done.

"Hey," he said, his eyes going to his brown oxfords before rising to meet mine. The cuffs of his pants were rolled once, and a patterned sock showed only just.

"Jesus, where did you come from?" I pressed a hand to both cheeks, trying to hide the heat in my face.

"I did some research . . . used your sketches as inspiration," he said as he took a step toward me, his voice lowering. "But here's the thing I don't understand . . ." He took another step.

"Mmmhmm?" I hummed, my breath caught in my throat. He'd used my sketches as inspiration?

"My cuffs," he said, holding his wrist up to me. "You see . . ." He took another step, his voice lowering to a whisper. "I'm supposed to cuff my shirt over the blazer, right?" He took another step.

"Yes," I said, my lips barely moving. He was close enough to kiss, and it was all I could think about.

I looked to Hudson and then to the floor, willing my cheeks to stop burning. He was making me foggy. He was making me sweat in places I shouldn't, considering the sheer ivory tank I wore underneath.

"But." He closed the space between us and leaned into me, his nose in my neck. "What do I do if I take my jacket off? Do I have to roll my sleeves again?" His breath hot against my skin. Every one of my senses was on high alert, and I loved it. Nothing else mattered in that moment. Not even the fact that we were standing in a semi-crowded lobby.

"And then what do I do when I put my jacket back on?" His lips grazed just under my ear as he spoke. "Do I have to unroll my cuffs, put my jacket on, and then recuff over the blazer?" He ran his thumb along my jawline, starting at my ear. He was electric.

I couldn't answer. My stomach was in my throat in the best way possible. I swallowed hard as he cupped my face with both hands.

"Hmm?" He trailed both thumbs down the side of my face and then linked his hands behind his back.

I blinked hard.

"What—" I couldn't form words. I couldn't process what was happening. What I was seeing. What I heard. What I felt.

"Edie, this is important. Can you please pay attention?" he teased. "My eyes are up here." Using two fingers he pointed to his eyes, then me.

I pressed my palms to my cheeks, my face burning.

"Come on, then," he said, offering me his arm. I linked mine through his, grasping his bicep as we began to move toward the theater entrance. "Let me know when you've regained your ability to speak."

"So, you really like my outfit?" Hudson asked as we settled into our seats in front of Serena and Michael.

"I did . . . I do . . . I love it," I said, rambling. Feeling like I wanted to confess my love for who was in the outfit as well. "*Qu'il est beau.*"

"*Tu es belle, aussi.*" He smiled at me appreciatively. "Where'd you learn that one?" He slid his hand into mine, interlocking our fingers.

"Wouldn't you like to know?" I teased.

Serena cleared her throat with a loud *ahem* as the lights began to dim. "Keep it PG, you two. There are people around."

I turned to Serena. "What does that mean?" I whispered.

She looked at me, unconvinced. "Like you don't know," she said, motioning with her chin toward Hudson. He turned and offered her a purposefully awkward wave. "The two of you are oozing sex right now."

I gasped and swatted at her as the curtain went up. "We are not," I said, whispering like a mom scolding her kid in public.

Serena swatted me back, looking at me and then Hudson. She laughed. "You really are, though."

I huffed, smiling as I leaned back into my seat, settling in against Hudson's arm.

He leaned into me, his nose touching my ear and his breath hot against my face. "I really would like to know. I'm impressed that you've been teaching yourself conversational phrases."

I smiled, pulling my shoulder to my ear to keep the goose bumps from spreading. "My repertoire grows larger every day I need to keep you on your toes, you know." I smiled as I turned my head, our cheeks touching.

"My *repertoire* grows when I'm around you, too." He pressed his smile into my neck before kissing it.

Another small *ahem* came from behind.

"Don't forget where we are right now," I said, settling back into my seat.

He didn't move, his lips still close to my ear. "I will never forget where we are right now," he said. "Or how you look." He turned his face toward the stage. "Or the way you make me feel."

I smiled at my feet and then at him. "I feel like I'm floating," I whispered, suddenly aware of how light I felt when I was with him. How unburdened I felt with him near. How it felt like this moment could last forever.

"When I'm around you, I'm always floating. I'm always in outer space."

When I turned my head, his eyes were already waiting for mine. I smiled, squeezing his hand.

"Oh my God." Serena leaned between us. "Knock. It. Off," she said through a smile as she tugged my hair, causing me to settle back in my seat.

27

A Kiss, to Kiss, We Are Kissing

The four of us stepped into the cold night. The play had been great, and Terrance's lighting was beautiful. We waited for a little while after the close, but I needed to get out of my heeled booties as soon as possible.

"I need to get away from the two of you," Serena said. She hopped down the four steps that led out of the building. "I mean, honestly." She turned toward us, looking up from the bottom of the stairs.

I shook my head, my hand snugly in Hudson's. "Shut up," I said, my face flushing.

"But seriously, though," Michael added, lifting a hand at

both of us. "I worked some major magic with these two, didn't I?" He joined Serena at the bottom of the stairs.

Serena looked at us and then at Michael. "Oh, sweetie, this was bound to happen. If anything, you just sped it up a tiny bit."

"All right," I said, holding the last word, embarrassment seeping out of my pores. Hudson squeezed my hand. "Maybe you two should go."

"Yeah, like back to Michael's, for example," Hudson added, his voice dripping with suggestion. He may as well have winked at his friend.

"Oh my God. Wow," Serena said with a curt wave, walking in the direction of Michael's car. "Oh-kay. Good night, then."

Michael gave a quick salute to Hudson before jogging to catch up to Serena.

"That was embarrassing," I said, sinking my face into his chest.

Hudson pressed his lips to my head. "It's okay, P.P." I felt his smile grow.

"I told you to stop calling me P.P." I pushed Hudson away from me as we headed toward my dorm.

He smiled big as he caught my hand in his. "But it suits you, and I really, really love the way you hate it."

"You love how much I hate it?" I asked, pulling him to a stop. I squeezed his hand as my stomach tumbled. He looked so good, and it was a beautiful night, and he'd draped his blazer over my shoulders before we left the building, even though my sweater was plenty warm. The night couldn't have gone better.

"I do," he said, swinging our hands.

"What part of me hating that name is your favorite?" I prodded.

We began walking again. "Well, for starters I love the way your cheeks get red and your eyes get squinty," he said, pulling me in and kissing my forehead. "And I love the way you push me or pinch me or squeeze my hand tight."

"I'll just have to start doing things you don't love, then," I countered.

"Impossible." He shook his head with determination.

"I'm sure there are a few things I could do that you wouldn't love." I smiled.

"Since we're headed back to your room, you can show me all the things I'll hate."

"Oh, are you under the impression that you're coming over?" I teased.

"I mean, we could easily just go to my room," he said. "But Stephen J. is there, so . . ."

I squeezed his hand, shoving him with my shoulder.

"And plus, Serena told me she was staying at Michael's *and* that I could spend the night *and* that I could eat all her Oreos."

"Liar," I said with a laugh. "Are you seriously trying to tell me that her reaction just now was entirely preplanned?"

He pulled me to a stop, my dorm a sidewalk and a set of stairs away. "Yes, that is what I'm telling you. One-hundred percent preplanned. She's a great actress, right?" He pulled me into him.

"You are such a liar," I said with a laugh.

"*En français*," he said, pressing his lips to mine.

I smiled against his. "*Menteur*."

"Bravo!" He kissed me hard once.

"*La fleur.*"

I ran my fingers down his abdomen as I thought, my head against his chest while he quizzed me.

"Flower," I said.

He kissed my head in response. "*Nous sommes allés*."

I didn't know this one.

"You smell great," I said, nuzzling my face into him, avoiding the vocab I didn't know.

"*Je sais*," he said. "*Nous sommes allés*."

"And you looked really good tonight at the show," I said, smiling into his chest. "You made me sweaty in inappropriate places."

"*Merci, d'avoir remarqué*," he said with a laugh, shaking

his head. He knew I was avoiding answering. "I would really like to explore that statement further, but first: *Nous sommes allés.*"

"*Le vin est bon,*" I replied, saying one of the few phrases I knew by heart. *The wine is good.*

"*C'est vrai! Nous sommes allés.*"

I tilted my head so I could see his face. He smiled down at me, though not amused by my avoidance.

"Spell it," I said, knowing that sometimes it helped to visualize words if I was having trouble understanding.

He spelled the words slowly. Punctuating the last letter with a kiss to my head.

"We went," I said, guessing but feeling confident.

"Bravo," he said, entwining our fingers over his midsection. "*Nous allons apprendre.*"

Oh, I knew this one. "We are learning," I said with a smile.

"We are going to learn," he corrected, but awarding me with a kiss to the head anyway. "*Faire des courses.*"

"Easy, shopping," I said, looking up at him.

"*Trop facile?* How about: *Prenez le temps de vivre?*"

Nope, didn't know that one. "It wasn't getting too easy. I take it back," I said with a laugh.

"It's what we are doing right now. *Prenez le temps de vivre,*" he repeated.

"About to make out?"

Hudson let out a long, thoughtful sigh as he contemplated my offer. "*Ça pourrait être très facilement prévu*, but no."

"Oh my God, I have no clue what you just said." I pinched his side. I knew *prévu*, that meant *to plan*, and I knew *très*, that meant *very*. But as for the first phrase I had no clue.

"Tell me what I just said, and we can make out," he said, shying away from another pinch.

"Impossible," I said with a pout.

"Which is impossible, you translating what I said, or us making out?"

"Us making out will never be impossible," I said. Hudson ran his hand through my hair, brushing it away from my forehead and stopping as he cupped my cheek. "Translating, on the other hand . . ."

"*En français.*"

"*Embrasser pas difficiler*," I said, trying my hardest to come up with something even relatively close, but coming up short. I managed *Kissing is not work*. But *kiss* as a noun, not a verb, like I had said in the quiet room when I was denied a kiss.

Hudson burst into laughter, his abdomen shaking as he laughed. "Do you even know what you just said?" He brushed tears from his eyes.

"Yes!" I said, faking offense. I thought I used what little

vocabulary I had effectively. "Can I at least get an A for effort?"

"Yes, babe, of course." He was still laughing when he pressed his lips to my forehead. I pushed up so that his lips would press against mine once, and then twice. He smiled against my kiss, laughing.

"If you don't stop laughing at me, I'll make sure I laugh at you next time you're most vulnerable," I teased, squeezing his inner thigh for emphasis.

He laughed again, recoiling from my squeeze. "Okay, okay. I surrender." He pulled me in, his lips on mine again, except he couldn't stop laughing.

"Are you sure?" I asked.

"Yes," he said with another laugh.

"Just go on and get it all out." I sighed, knowing that this was a losing battle. Once he really got laughing it was all over.

Hudson let go, laughing fully, his belly shaking as he repeated the words I said in French. Laughing harder each time he repeated them.

I waited, crossing my arms as I watched his laughter finally start to fade. "Are you finished?" I asked.

He smiled, nodding.

"Good," I said, uncrossing my arms and running my finger over a tiny hole in his T-shirt. "How did you manage this?"

He looked down. "Stop playing with it; you'll make it bigger." He swatted my hand away playfully.

"But how did it even happen? How do you have all these tiny holes in your T-shirts?" I asked, finding another one closer to the hem.

"My cat, probably," he said, swatting my hand away again.

I laughed, hard. "Your cat did not do this," I said, swiping at the tears in my eyes. "There's no way."

"Yes, way," he said.

I touched the first hole again, laughing harder as I poked it.

"I guess I'll wait for you to be done," he said, crossing his arms.

I breathed deeply, letting out one more burst of laughter. I wiped my eyes with the inside of my wrist, smudging my mascara. I sighed loudly as I ran a fingertip under each eye, collecting any stray black smears.

"Have I told you today how beautiful you are?"

"More or less," I said, wiping my finger on his shirt. "Stop stalling. I need to study."

"Have I told you how much I like being around you?"

"Again, more or less." I rolled my eyes with a smirk. He gently ran his thumb from my temple to my chin and then down my neck.

"Have I told you that I think I'm falling in love with you?"

My breath caught in my throat. "Uh, nope. You have not mentioned that."

"Oh, well, Edie, I think you should know that I am falling in love with you."

I searched his eyes. I knew he'd wanted to say it; I just wasn't as prepared to hear it as I thought I would be.

"Are you serious?" I breathed.

"I'm seriously serious."

"Seriously?" I asked again, unable to believe him. Shocked by his sudden sincerity. "How do you—"

"Yes, seriously."

"But h-how—" I stuttered, unsure of what to say.

"First of all, I just know. You took care of me, and that means a lot." His thumbs brushed my temples as he sighed. "That means something to me. You mean something to me."

"And you think that something is love?"

"It could be," he said, though I knew he was sure.

"Say it in German," I teased.

"*Ich glaube ich liebe dich.*"

"Say it in Spanish," I said, the heat in my cheeks spreading down my neck.

"*Puede ser amor.*"

"Say it in French," I whispered.

"*Ça pourrait bien être l'amour,*" he said as he pressed his lips to mine.

28

A Picture Says a Thousand Uh-Ohs

"I don't know, maybe I'll just come back at the end of the summer," I said with a shrug, my eyes on the court.

I glanced at Terrance when he didn't immediately respond, his mouth hanging open. "What?" I asked.

"Are you seriously considering not doing the fall semester all of a sudden?" he asked, his thumb scrolling his phone as he gawked at me.

I shrugged again.

He whistled, low and long. "You've got it bad," he said, his eyes leaving my face and returning to his cell.

I pulled back. "Got it bad for what?" I asked, my attention

grabbed by the referee's whistle. "What just happened?" I motioned toward the court as Terrance's eyes stayed on his phone.

"No clue," he said, setting his phone on the bleacher next to him.

"Oh," I said, watching Serena ready her serve. "Out of bounds, them."

Terrance nodded, resting his feet on the seat below. He leaned forward, his elbows sliding onto his thighs.

"I know I've already told you this—the play was awesome. I loved your lighting; it was gorgeous," I said, bumping into him.

"Thanks," he said, tilting his head to look at me. "I'm surprised you saw any of it, though." He smirked.

"What does that mean?" I asked, watching the other team volley the ball.

"I heard about you and Hudson."

I scrunched my nose as I glanced his way. "What does *that* mean?" I asked with more emphasis.

"It means I heard you were more interested in Hudson than you were in the show." A smile creeped at the left side of his mouth.

"Oh my God," I said, shoving him lightly.

"And now it seems like you're more interested in Hudson than Paris—"

"Uh, no," I interrupted, my stomach dropping in the process.

"Uh, yeah," he said. "You literally just said you were thinking about coming home at the end of the summer. That was never the plan. Regardless of the question, the answer was always Paris."

I scratched my head, avoiding eye contact with Terrance, despite his desperate attempt to grab my gaze.

"Am I wrong?" he asked, giving up on trying to make eye contact.

I took a long sip from my water bottle. He wasn't wrong. The answer to any question had been Paris. It was supposed to stay that way, too.

"Can we just watch the game?" I motioned to the court.

He shook his head slowly. "Whatever you want, Edie."

I sat staring at the computer screen. Fifty-nine. The grade on my last French test. It didn't make sense. I studied for this test. I really studied. I sank my head into my hands as the room door opened behind me.

"What's up?" Serena asked, setting her bag down hard.

I shook my head. What was there to say?

"What happened?" she asked, crossing the room to stand over my shoulder. "Oh."

"Yeah."

"Your overall grade is still a sixty-five, so that's good." Her fingertip pressed the screen. "You can recoup."

I laughed as I lifted my face from my hands. I rubbed the heels of my hands into my eyes. "I'm not going to make it through this course," I said, pushing out of the chair and moving to my bed.

"You will. You're passing," she said, turning to unpack her bag.

I fell back onto the bed, throwing an arm over my face.

"Hey, so I have something to show you," Serena said as she shuffled through some papers.

"Okay," I said, not taking my arm off my eyes.

She moved to the side of my bed. "Did you want to see it, or . . . ?"

I groaned as I pulled my arm from my face, dropping it dramatically onto the bed next to me.

Serena waved for me to sit up.

"Do I have to?"

She listed her head, her hand on her hip as she looked down at me.

"Fine," I whined as I pushed myself up. I opened my arms as if to present myself.

"So, I was going through my pictures." She held her tablet toward me. "Selecting pictures and editing and whatever, and I found these. . . ." She handed me the tablet. The first picture was of me sitting at my desk, my dress pooled in my lap. My face downcast, smiling. A pin between my lips.

I flipped to the next. And then another. "What are these?" I asked as I got to a picture that instantly knotted my stomach.

It was me and Hudson. Nose to nose at the theater. Serena must have snapped it right before she scolded us. His fingers twisted in the end of my hair, my mouth open in a smile.

I looked up at Serena, her eyebrows raised in response. There was a picture of us walking away from Serena. Hudson with his hands shoved into his pockets, my arm looped through his. My head on his shoulder.

"What is this?" I asked, holding the tablet toward her.

She laughed as she ran a hand through her hair. "That's you falling in love with Wes Hudson."

"Jesus . . ." I dropped the tablet. "There have to be more than twenty pictures on there."

"Twenty-seven, actually," Serena said, biting the inside of her cheek. "It's a really beautiful progression, Edie, and I—"

I looked up at her. "You want to use those for your project now instead of the dress pictures?"

She paused, still chewing on the inside of her cheek. She raised her eyebrows questioningly.

"I promise I will still take pictures for your portfolio," Serena said, flipping through her tablet and turning it toward me to show me a photo of me pulling out a hem. "I still have so many good pictures of you with The Dress."

I rubbed my hands down my face. "Do you think the pictures stand a chance to get the gallery spot?" I asked.

Serena shifted her weight from one foot to the other. "I do."

"Shit," I breathed.

"It's totally up to you, Edie," she said, crossing her arms. "I promised you final say, and I meant it."

I nodded. "Yeah, I know," I said. "Just go with your gut." I fell back onto my bed.

"You're sure?"

I nodded, throwing my arms over my eyes again.

"Do you want to see the rest of the pictures? You only saw, like, three pictures; there are a lot—"

"Nope," I interrupted. I did not want to see the rest of the pictures. "I trust you," I said. It was myself that I didn't trust. How could I have allowed Hudson to derail me like this?

29

This Misery Does Not Love Your Company, fyi

We'd agreed to meet in Hudson's room to study. One, because I didn't want an audience for this conversation and I knew Serena would want to be there, camera at the ready. And two, because it was easier to walk away than it was to ask him to leave, in so many ways.

I would be lying if I said I didn't have a pit in my stomach over this. I didn't want to end things with Hudson, but I had to. I'd gotten in too deep and broken all my rules. What we'd had was fun. It was supposed to stay fun. It was supposed to stay easy, not get in the way of everything else going on in my life . . . but it did and now it had to end.

Hudson's head was down, my notebook rested in his lap. I watched him as he ran a finger over the words I'd written, reading them. Checking for any mistakes.

"You know, when I'm in Paris, I don't think . . . you know, we need to be . . ." I motioned between us, using it as the end of the sentence.

Hudson narrowed his eyes. "You don't think we need to be . . . ?"

"Like, a thing," I said, not wanting to use the word *couple*. Or *boyfriend*. Or *girlfriend*. Or *relationship*. Not wanting any of those words.

He sat up straight, his palms pressed into the bed. "Are you preemptively breaking up with me?" he asked, his eyes shining in the soft light of his room. He bit at his bottom lip, holding back a smile.

I opened my mouth to respond, but closed it before I could say something stupid. I shook my head, trying to sort my thoughts.

"Oh my God," he said, pulling back. His face falling. "You are, aren't you?"

"Hudson, I just thought—"

His eyebrows knitted together before I could finish my sentence. "You thought what? That this thing between us was going to stay *cool*, as you put it?" he said, using air quotes.

"Hudson, no." I pushed out of the chair and stood in front of him. "I still need you. I still need help—"

"Why am I even helping you, Edie?" he asked, tossing my notebook toward me. "So you can leave the country and not think about me again until you return?"

"That's not what I meant," I said, though it was kind of what I'd meant, but also he was absolutely getting in the way of me passing French when he was meant to get me through it.

He pressed his fingers into his eyes, inhaling deeply through his nose. "Don't do this, Edie," he said, taking another deep breath before looking up at me.

"Hudson, I—"

"It doesn't have to be all or nothing."

I closed my eyes. Maybe it didn't have to be all or nothing, but it had to be over.

"I still want to see you. I don't want this to be over."

I crossed my arms, holding myself together. I didn't want it to be over, either, not really, but I had other priorities. There was no way I was going to let myself make Hudson a priority over all the things I'd worked so hard to achieve.

"You knew it would be like this," I started to say, stopping when Hudson pushed off the bed. "And we aren't *breaking up*, I mean, we aren't even really together."

He crossed his arms. "What do you mean we aren't really together? And be like what? That you would fall for me and then run away? No, actually I didn't know it would be like that."

I shook my head. That wasn't what I'd meant. Sure, I'd fallen for him, but in my head, there was always an end date. A time stamp. "I don't have time for this, Hudson. I need to pass the final, and I need you to help me. This is why I didn't want a boyfriend. . . . This is why I told you that I just needed you as a tutor."

He let his head fall back, his eyes on the ceiling. "You've been using me," he said with a realization that overtook him. He righted his head, any glimmer in his eyes gone.

"I never used you," I said, my finger pointed in his direction. I took a deep breath before I spoke again. "I'm sorry if it came off that way."

"I get why you're pushing me away right now, but it doesn't have to be like this—"

I put my hand up to stop him. "Hudson, I don't have time for conversations like this, either."

He took a step back, his forehead scrunched. "Are you serious right now?" he asked, his voice rising.

I opened my mouth to respond, but he jumped in.

"You don't have time to talk to me about something you brought up? Something that's your issue, not mine? Edie, this is bullshit."

I picked at my cardigan, dropping mustard yellow puffs to the floor.

"Just tell me what's really going on, please?"

I shook my head. What was really going on was that I

didn't want to regret going to Paris. I didn't want anything holding me back. I didn't want to split my time between my dream and a boy.

"This is how it is," I said, taking my notebook off the bed and putting it into my bag. "My priority is to pass this class and go to Paris." I hiked my tote onto my shoulder. "I'm sorry, but I don't plan on changing that anytime soon."

I'd slept an exhausted sleep. A sleep that only comes after you've been broken down past the point of no return. I slept a sleep that didn't refresh me. I slept a sleep that left me filled with dread that only deepened when I woke. Dread I'd brought on myself. The conversation with Hudson hadn't ended when I left his room. He'd texted me twice, both times trying to justify why we should stay together. Telling me that he wasn't going anywhere. That he would be there for me when I came around. The problem was that I had no intention of coming around.

I walked into class just as it started. I was no longer going to show up ten minutes early. I walked to the front of the classroom and set the transmitter on the table, not bothering to look at either Dr. Clément or Hudson. I hated that I still needed him. I hated that I was teetering on a D and needed every moment of this lecture. I hated that I could feel his eyes on me.

I slid into my seat, taking a deep breath as I pulled out my notebook and slipped the earpiece onto my ear.

"I miss you," he whispered.

I kept my eyes on my desk and shook my head.

"Edie, I—"

I pulled the earpiece out of my ear and dropped it on my desk. I couldn't listen to him. I couldn't do this.

I needed at least a sixty-five on the final to pass the class. That sixty-five may as well have been a hundred at this rate. I felt less confident than ever, and the pressure was on full force. I no longer had the luxury of studying with the TA. I no longer had the luxury of knowing someone had my back, either.

I stayed in my seat as the room cleared. I needed to get the transmitter back, and I felt like such a fool. This was more embarrassing than anything that had happened to me in middle school. This was worse than any teasing that was dished out by my classmates.

Hudson set the transmitter on my desk, and I kept my eyes down. I didn't want to look at him. I didn't want him to see me, either.

"Edie, just—can we talk?" he pleaded.

"I warned you," I said, finally looking into his eyes. He

looked like he'd slept the same exhausted sleep as me. He looked like he'd been through hell. He was disheveled in all the worst ways. He wasn't even wearing his maroon beanie. His shirt was wrinkled. He was in sweatpants. Actual athletic sweatpants.

He took a step back so that I could pass him. His eyes begging for me to reconsider. I held it together until I was out of the building, but couldn't keep the tears from coming once I was in the light of day.

Only five more French classes until the semester ended. Only five more interactions with him. Only five more heartbreaks.

Paris, Paris, Paris, I reminded myself.

30

It Matters How This Ends

Serena and I walked arm in arm toward the arts building. My insides quaked, torn between not wanting to see myself in those photos and wanting to support my best friend.

"You are way too dressed up for this," Serena said as she eyed my heeled booties, skinny jeans, and plum-colored cashmere V-neck. "As my date, I feel as though I have to tell you this."

I cleared my throat. "I am not." I ran my hand against my sweater. "This is a special occasion, and I think one should dress accordingly . . . and I'm only your date because Michael is taking a final."

"But you're still my date." Serena laughed. "And I should be the one dressing accordingly, but you're just a spectator."

"I am not just a spectator," I said, pulling her to a stop. "I'm featured in these photographs and I want my best self represented."

"You want your best self represented even when you're not featured," she laughed, pulling me toward the building.

"I like dressing up," I said.

"I know. You'd get all dressed up to do something like go to Pizza Hut for dinner or play checkers in a park."

I smiled at my roommate despite my annoyance. She knew me too well. My idea of a perfect date included being impeccably dressed and doing something totally normal. I'd even made her get dressed up to go out to the movies a couple times.

"Like the time I desperately wanted to go to Trader Joe's for the squishy penguin gummies and you wouldn't go with me unless I wore that gray boatneck sweater and pink chiffon skirt?"

"First of all, it wasn't *pink*, it was champagne . . . and it wasn't *gray*, it was smoke; and secondly, it was gorgeous and you looked amazing, so whatever," I said, flicking my wrist at her commentary.

The gallery was packed, and between the photographs and the buzz of low conversation, all my attention was occupied as I moved slowly from one photo to the next. It was impossible to deny what Serena had captured, falling in love. A feeling so many have tried to explain through words and art and dance, but for me never quite hit the mark. But these photos hit the mark. It was all over my face in every picture. My body language. My hands. My eyes. Everything aglow with new love.

New love.

I stopped at a photo I had seen earlier in the week, the one with my dress pooled in my lap, pins in my mouth. That was who I was. The Edie who had dreams, ideas, goals yet achieved. I'd snipped away a piece of that Edie to make room for Hudson. Carefully trimming my edges and serging him in without even realizing it.

I let my head fall forward, closing my eyes. It was all too much. The movement. The whispered conversations. The heating system blowing. The glass doors whooshing every time someone entered the gallery.

"Edie."

I turned to see Cody. "I called your name like three times," he said.

"Oh, hey," I said, looking at my feet. He probably had,

but there was too much going on in the gallery for me to focus. "Sorry." I waved my hand around. "You know."

He nodded, rocking back on his heels. He snapped his fingers, clapping his hand against his fist. "So," he said, motioning to a portrait of me, my face illuminated by my cell phone, a slow smile on my face.

I released a sharp breath. "Yeah." I looked at the portrait. It was the riddle text conversation. The *wet umbrella* pun. I turned back to Cody with a shrug.

He shook his head, turning to look at the picture behind us. The one of Hudson and me nose to nose in the theater. "I just—"

"Cody," I started.

"No." He put up his hand. "Edie, I just feel like things could have been different between us."

I breathed unevenly, my shoulder slumping forward. I shook my head. "Maybe."

"Yeah . . . ," he said, crossing his arms. "So, did you, uh, do the same thing to this poor kid?" He rubbed the back of his neck before returning his arm to the crossed position.

I blinked. "No," I lied. "It wasn't like that."

He nodded, his eyes wandering to the other photos of me. "So, you and he were never a thing?"

"We weren't supposed to be," I said, trying to convince myself.

"But you and I, we were a thing," he said, his eyes meeting mine.

I nodded. Cody and I had been a thing. I'd never put a title on it. In fact, I'd gone out of my way to not put a title on it. We didn't go on dates, we hung out. We weren't seeing each other. We weren't friends with benefits. He was exactly what I wanted him to be . . . an arm's length away, but within reach.

He pressed his lips together "Well, thanks for finally admitting to that," he said.

I let my head fall back, focusing on the ceiling fans above, cycling out of sync.

"It's just that it would have been easier if you actually broke up with me, you know?" he said. When I looked at him, his eyes were down.

"Instead of just an 'It's over' text. If you'd had the balls to tell me the truth." His voice was barely a whisper.

"I should never have done that," I said, guilt filling my stomach. There I was, surrounded by pictures of me and Hudson, talking to Cody about how our non-relationship relationship crapped out before it could even begin. "I'm sorry."

Cody laughed, forced and harsh. "You're sorry?"

I winced.

"You break up with me, for all intents and purposes, and

then ghost me for weeks." He put his hands on his hips. "Dead air for days, like I never even existed to you, and then when you do reach out it's nonsense."

It was all true, but it was for a reason.

"Listen, all I want to say is that if I were this guy"—he motioned toward a picture of me and Hudson—"I wouldn't let you go. I'd fight to the death for you. I'd fight until you were on the plane, taking off into the air."

I took a step back.

"Hey, you two," Serena said, resting her arms on my shoulders. "Everything okay?"

"Yeah," Cody said. "We're good. I was actually just about to leave." He motioned over his shoulder with his thumb.

I forced a smile, wrapping my arms around my middle.

"Well, thanks for coming," Serena said, gracious as always. "I hope you, uh—liked it . . . ?"

Cody shoved his hands into his pockets. "You did a great job, Serena. Congrats." He smiled at her before turning away.

The moment Cody was out of sight Serena turned to me. "What was that?" she asked through a forced smile.

"How much did you hear?" I asked, running my hand through my hair.

"It wasn't so much what I heard, it was more like what I saw. Your body language and his."

I huffed, dropping my folded arms. "Well, whatever it was that you saw, I deserved."

"How do you figure?" Serena asked. "Just like you don't owe Hudson anything, you don't owe Cody anything, either. At least with Cody you were more upfront from the beginning. . . . He just thought he'd change your mind."

"He sure did," I said, rolling my eyes at the memory of him asking me not to go to Paris and to spend the summer with him at his family's place in Martha's Vineyard.

"Listen, as much as I don't want to see you hurting, you have a right to make your own choices. If Paris is the priority, which we all know it is, then that's it. I respect that . . . but it doesn't have to be black and white."

"That's basically what Hudson said."

She gestured with her hands. "See?"

"That doesn't mean he's right . . . or that you are."

She turned to me, her hands on her hips. "You *can* live without Wesley Hudson. I have no doubt about that. But you don't *have* to. You don't have to let it end like this. It matters how this ends, Edie. It matters because there will be life after French 102 and Paris in the fall. Give yourself a break, okay? Get out of the *right now* and think about the *after* for a second."

31

D Stands for Done

"Why do I have more confidence in you than you do?" Serena asked as we sat at a table in the back of the tutoring center.

Ha. Story of my life right here. I had little to no confidence in my ability to pass this final exam. Passing this exam meant I would pass the course. A sixty-five on this exam meant a sixty-five in French 102.

D meant *done* as far as I was concerned.

I didn't feel confident in what I'd learned. I didn't feel confident that I could get through the final with a sixty-five. I wasn't confident in myself at all. I felt so totally knocked down and dragged out. I wasn't confident in Hudson's original strategy of focusing on the vocab and not on the listening. I wasn't confident that I would finish on time. I wasn't confident that I could keep my attention off Hudson and on the test.

"There is so much pressure to pass this. I literally feel like I'm dying," I said as I opened my hand to her and received three penguin gummies in return. I popped them all into my mouth at once.

"Are you sure that feeling isn't from everything going on with you and Hudson?" she asked.

I may have still been upset with him, but passing French was the priority. Passing French was the most important hurdle. I couldn't even consider making things right with him until I knew my French fate. And I did plan on making things right with him. Something inside me said that time would help. That I could take the time I needed to figure out a balance. That maybe we could move forward as friends.

"Honestly, I can't even with him right now. This is my priority. This is where my head needs to be," I said, tapping my stack of flash cards. Except my head was not on French, it was exactly where Serena said it was: on Hudson.

I sighed as I followed her lead and started gathering all my study materials.

"So, I got this thing," Serena said, biting at her bottom

lip as she swiped at her phone. "And I think you should see it."

I dropped a handful of highlighters into my bag as I watched her.

"It's, um—" She handed me the phone. "Just read it."

I held her eyes as I took her phone, swallowing hard before looking at the screen.

HUDSON: Your photo series was incredible. You deserved to win.

HUDSON: I should have told you when I was at the gallery, but I couldn't bring myself to talk to you, sorry.

          SERENA: Thank you

          SERENA: It's ok. I understand.

HUDSON: Is it possible for me to have copies of those pics?

          SERENA: Of course

HUDSON: I guess I'm a glutton for punishment

          SERENA: Just so you know, she is, too

HUDSON: I saw that you had the collection titled "Falling in Love," but may I suggest a different title?

SERENA: Haha. Yeah, real creative.
I know. Sure.

HUDSON: Avec la douleur
exquise

SERENA: You're gonna make me
google that, aren't you?

"What does it mean?" I asked.

Serena shrugged as she extended her hand to take her phone back. "Google Translate was no help. I thought maybe we could ask Makenna," she said, throwing a look over her shoulder.

I pursed my lips as I watched Makenna working on the computer, her back to us.

"Can you translate something for us?" I asked Makenna, nodding to Serena to hand Makenna the phone.

"Yeah, of course." Makenna looked at it and then up to me. A small smile started in the corner of her mouth and then spread to take over her whole face. "Who wrote this, Hudson?"

I nodded.

She shook her head, blushing as she looked at the phone again. My eyes went to Serena and then back to Makenna.

"I tried to google it, but it didn't translate to anything that actually made sense. 'With exquisite pain'?" Serena said.

"No, it wouldn't," she said, handing back the phone.

"*Avec la douleur exquise* literally translates to exquisite pain, yes, but that doesn't really do it justice. It comes from the medical word for a pain that opiates can't even dull. In life and love, it's used to describe the indescribable pain of knowing you cannot have the person you love."

I looked from Makenna to Serena. I could see it in both of their faces. They were both swooning.

"Stop," I warned Serena, knowing she was going to use this as yet another reason for me to get on with it and make up with Hudson . . . and potentially as a name for the collection. Considering the circumstances, it was a fitting name, I had to give him that.

"Can I be honest for, like, one second?" Makenna asked, interrupting the silent conversation I was having with Serena.

I shrugged. "Sure," I said, knowing that there was pretty much nothing she could say that could make this situation any more awkward.

"I don't know if Huds told you this or not, but I asked him out last semester," she said. "We went on a couple dates, but it didn't work out, obviously."

I nodded slowly, wondering where she was going with this.

"This isn't him."

"What do you mean?" Serena asked, since I wasn't quick enough.

"I mean, he must really be in deep with you, because the

Hudson I know would never have written something like this. He never would have opened up like that," she said, her eyes moving from me to some point over my left shoulder. "Trust me."

32

Angel Wings

We were one hour into the final, and my eyes met Hudson's for the third time. He openly watched me. Not like he hadn't been watching me these past few weeks anyway, but seeing him watch me now made me sad. He was worried about me, that much was clear.

I didn't regret the time we'd spent goofing around instead of studying. What I did regret was allowing myself to be distracted from the beginning. Hudson was a distraction. At the end of the day, that was what our relationship boiled down to. Maybe I pursued him on purpose. Self-sabotage. If

I failed, I could blame him. If Paris didn't work out that summer, I could blame him.

"*Il vous reste trente minutes, mesdames et messieurs.*"

Dr. Clément's voice came through my earpiece, startling the crap out of me. His announcement that we had thirty minutes left to complete the exam initiated nearly half the class to rise from their seats, declaring silently that they were already done.

Except this part of test taking was never a silent declaration. I heard everything. Every chair scrape. Every shuffled paper. Every whispered *how do you think you did*. This very moment was the exact reason I used to take my tests in a separate location in high school.

I put my pen down and waited. There was no sense in trying to finish until the herd had handed in their booklets and left. I looked at Hudson. He was watching me again as he bit his bottom lip.

I couldn't focus on him right now. I had to focus on the rest of my test. I had to get as many of the multiple-choice questions correct as possible.

"You have five minutes to finish up, Edie."

Dr. Clément's voice was soft in my ear. I looked up. Why was he only addressing me?

Oh.

I was the only person still in the 100-seat lecture hall.

And I still had an entire page to go. I was done for. This was over. I'd be back in this room in the fall.

I'd kept up the best I could during the listening section. I'd gotten through the vocab and the fill-in-the-blanks and even the adjectives, but the reading section was killing me. The reading section was about to do me in.

I breathed slowly. I still had five minutes. A lot could happen in five minutes. I could get something done in five minutes, get through the rest of this test.

I stared at the few words I'd written on the page. It wasn't nearly enough. It wasn't quality and it wasn't enough.

"You can do this," Hudson whispered in my ear. "Forget about the time, and focus."

I shook my head, my eyes on the nearly blank page. I wasn't going to make it.

"No to which?" he asked. "The *you can do this* or the *forget about the time, and focus*?"

I looked up at him. Actually looked at him for the first time in over three weeks. I looked at the way he watched me. The way his eyes told me I could do it. How he genuinely wanted me to beat this test.

"Both," I said aloud, closing my test and sinking my head back into my hands.

"Edie, don't—" he started, but I pulled the earpiece before he could finish.

The exam scores wouldn't be posted until midnight. I checked my phone for the ninth time, and only five minutes had passed. I still had two hours to go.

"I really want to see The Dress," Serena nagged for the third time. "Can we just go see The Dress?"

I stared at the Word document on my laptop. I had an essay to write, three casual beachwear outfit designs to finish, and the last chapter of a book for British Lit. Just because French was done and over with didn't mean I was in the clear for all my other classes, but going to visit my dress had enough pull for me to forget about everything else.

Serena sat on her desk, her legs swinging as she watched me.

I sighed as I closed my laptop.

"Yay!" she cheered as she hopped off her desk. She ferociously shoved her feet into her boots. "Come on, come on."

"Oh my God." I laughed as I slipped into my Keds and pulled on my wool coat. "You are out of control right now."

"I can't wait another second to see this dress, Edie. It's all you've talked about for, like, ever. There are sketches of it all around the room. You even talk about it in your sleep." She opened the door and waved me through.

"I'm sure I don't talk about it in my sleep."

"You definitely do," she said as she shoved me lightly with her shoulder.

It was Grecian. This was in all senses of the term navy blue, but as it moved in the light you saw hints of teal and bronze. It was modeled after one I'd seen on a beautiful actress at an awards show when I was ten. She'd worn it with such grace that I knew I had to have it, and at that time fashion wasn't a living, breathing thing for me. I kept that image in my mind anyway, storing it until I decided to look it up on the internet when I'd finally dived headfirst into patterning and sewing.

The entire dress was draped, which was a style of construction that meant I'd spent hours standing at the dress form, moving and shifting fabric. Pinning and unpinning. Pricking myself and trying to keep drops of blood off the fabric.

Instead of a traditional belt made of woven rope, this had a stylized structured belt. Cinched at the waist and split up the side seams to form the straps—bridle straps, similar to the way a shoulder holster for a gun would look. The top of the bodice then connected to the straps at the center of the sternum. This formed a soft diamond shape to complete the look of the front of the bodice. It had a plunging back, which meant my back was completely bare. Any lower and the top of my butt crack might have shown.

"It truly looks beautiful," Serena said as she stood a few steps back over my left shoulder.

The Dress was done and I couldn't believe it. She'd asked to be there for the grand reveal, which was perfect because I needed someone to zip me up. Double plus, I needed a distraction from the two-hour wait I had until my final grade for French would be posted. Triple plus, Serena was still taking pictures for my portfolio.

"It's certainly been a labor of love," I said, making eye contact with her in the full-length mirror. "You like the color?"

"I love the color," Serena said, taking a step closer to me. "You know that."

It was a conversation we'd had over and over last year when I was choosing the fabric. I'd dragged Serena into the lab and made her look through boxes and boxes of fabrics. She wanted to see me in something closer to the original color, something in the green family, but once I saw this navy I was sold.

I ran my fingers over the centerpiece, the belt, iridescent in whites, purples, blues. It was stiff, the backed Lycra smooth against my fingertips. The individual pieces affixed to gold cording.

"I love this texture, too," she said, taking another step toward me. She ran her fingers over the strap, starting at my shoulder and then down my shoulder blade, stopping at my side. "It looks like feathers, or snakeskin, or, I don't know . . . a fancy purse."

I laughed, looking down at my bare toes as The Dress pooled around my feet. It was a bit long, made to be worn with high heels, but of all the fashion choices in all the world, high heels were my least favorite. I wiggled my toes before meeting Serena's eyes in the mirror. I wasn't supposed to be barefoot in the shop; it was a rule. Professor Sheelan didn't want to hear anyone complaining about stepping on a stray straight pin or sharp button or, God help you, a four-inch safety pin.

Serena touched my shoulder again, her fingertip gliding against the strap. "These look like wings, you know." She smiled. "Like angel wings."

"I was hoping they would," I said, delighted as I pulled my shoulder up and pressed my cheek into the right one. "I just can't believe it's finished."

"I can. You've worked your butt off on this," Serena said as her phone chimed across the room. She moved toward her bag. "I know this semester was hard for you, and you spent a lot of time doubting yourself, but just look at yourself now. Look at what you made . . ."

She trailed off as she checked her phone. Her thumbs tapped quickly before she looked back up at me.

"The next time something is hard, the next time you find yourself thinking you are anything other than completely brilliant, remember this moment, right now." She pointed at me, her cell in her hand. It chimed again. "Remember the way you feel having accomplished this. Forget the fact that you look like a friggin' supermodel right now." She laughed as she checked her phone. "Just remember that this is your calling."

"Thank you," I said with a nod.

Serena's phone chimed again.

"Something wrong?" I asked as I watched her check her phone for the third time. Her eyebrows knitted together.

"Um," she said, her eyes on the phone as her thumbs tapped. "It's Hudson." Her eyes slowly met mine in the mirror.

"What about Hudson?" I asked, bristling slightly. I gathered the skirt with both hands and walked toward the dressing room. "I'm going to need you to unzip me."

"There's no time," she said, her eyes full of urgency. "We have to go."

Have to go? I repeated in my head.

"What do you mean we have to go?" I dropped the skirt and moved toward her.

"He needs us," she said, holding the phone up, the screen lit, but I couldn't read anything written. "We have to go."

"He needs us for what?" I said, feeling a panic rise inside me. "Is he okay? Oh my God . . ."

"I think he's okay, for now. But he needs us, like, now. Apparently, he's been texting you, too."

I touched my sides, feeling for my phone in the pockets

243

I'd hidden in the layers of silk and crepe. It was a personal touch, something, stylistically, I believed should be built into every dress. Men got to have pockets at all times; why couldn't women?

I pulled my phone out, and sure enough, I had eight missed texts.

> **HUDSON:** Meet me at Fay. Asap
>
> **HUDSON:** I need you.
>
> **HUDSON:** I mean, I need your help.
>
> **HUDSON:** Please, Edie. Pleeeaaasssseeee.
>
> **HUDSON:** S'il vous plaît
>
> **HUDSON:** Por favor
>
> **HUDSON:** Bitte
>
> **HUDSON:** Per favore

I looked at Serena. I rolled my eyes with a sigh. There was no way this was an emergency. I knew Hudson well enough to know this was something else. Part of me wanted to play along because clearly he was planning something, him and Serena.

"Seriously?" I asked.

"What did he say to you?" she asked, keeping up the facade of urgency.

I listed my head and put my hands on my hips. "This is obviously some ploy the two of you are in on," I said, waving one hand in her direction before placing it back on my hip.

"Edie, I don't think this is some ploy," Serena said, holding her phone up again, the screen lit, but again I couldn't read anything on it. "Can you just get your shoes on, please?"

I sighed as I turned from her. "I'm going to change."

"Edie—"

I turned back toward her, the tone of her voice catching me in the stomach. Maybe this was serious. I searched her eyes, examined her body language, looked at the grip her hand had on the cell phone.

"You're serious?" I asked.

She nodded, motioning toward my shoes, which sat by the door.

"It's freezing out. I'm going to freeze to death if I go out like this," I said as I moved toward the door, my dress fisted in each hand. I slipped into my yellow Keds, cringing at the look of this dress with those shoes.

"Here," Serena said, tossing me my cranberry peacoat.

"You can't be serious," I said, holding it in one hand while the other held the skirt off the floor.

"*You* can't be serious," she said back, knowing full well that my issue was with the clashing colors.

I heaved a great sigh as I pulled the coat on, flipping up

the collar to protect from the wind I knew would immediately freeze both of us.

We scurried across campus to the science building, a building that we both prayed had the heat on full blast.

Serena in sweatpants tucked into sheepskin boots in the traditional tan color everyone had and me in a dress better suited for a gala than for a hike across campus in the wind and rain. We looked ridiculous.

"Why Fay Hall?" I asked as we stepped into the building.

"How am I supposed to know?" she asked, running her fingers through her hair, trying to get out the knots the wind had caused.

I did the same as I looked around the building. I hadn't been in there since first semester freshman year when I took the obligatory science class for nonscience majors.

I unbuttoned my coat and fished my phone out of my dress pocket.

ME: D'accord. We're here.

I looked up at Serena to see her staring at me. She took a step toward me as my phone buzzed in my hand.

HUDSON: 4th floor. Room 414.

"Fourth floor," I said, my eyes on the phone and then up to her. She was standing right in front of me.

"Let me just . . ." She brushed a few stray pieces of hair behind my ear, tilting her head as she looked me over.

I took a step back. "What are you doing?" I asked, moving toward the bank of elevators.

"Can I just . . ." She reached out to smooth down my hair on the left side. "Okay, there. And give me that." She tugged at my coat.

"Give you my coat? Why?" I asked as I shrugged it off anyway.

She smiled, sighing with her hand out, palm up.

I handed her the coat. "This is a setup. What have the two of you concocted?"

"Just go," she said, her smile consuming her face as she called for the elevator.

The elevator dinged open as I spoke. "I hate you a little right now."

"Let me know if you feel the same in a few hours," she said, stepping back as the elevator doors closed.

33

And the Stars Look Very Different Today

Hudson stood in the hallway, his back pressed to the wall and his face toward the ceiling, waiting. I paused to take him in before stepping out of the elevator, my breath catching in my throat. He was in a suit. Why was he in a suit?

"Hey," I said. I felt my stomach flip as his head snapped in my direction.

"Hey." He smiled his megawatt smile as he pushed off the wall to face me. I felt my entire body flush as he took me in. He was in a black tuxedo. A full-on bow tie and cummerbund tuxedo, both accessories in navy blue.

"Room four-fourteen?" I asked, motioning to the open doorway to his right.

"Unofficially," he said. His words coming out breathy as he watched me. I could feel his eyes as they skimmed my body. Took in my bare shoulders, my exposed back . . . potentially the top of my butt crack. "Come on, you made it just in time."

"Hudson," I said as I moved past him and toward the open doorway, my dress gathered in each hand to keep it from dragging. "Why am I here?"

He searched my face. His eyes not leaving mine. "Can you just come with me?" His hands were in his pockets, and he twisted his wrist to see his watch. "Just trust me, okay?"

I dropped my dress to pull out my phone. I still had an hour until grades would be posted. "Yeah." I nodded. "Okay."

"*Après toi.*" He smiled, ushering me in.

After you. I hesitated as I translated in my head, watching his face before moving. His eyes were just as I remembered. Blue and gray and beautiful, and looking into them now was the answer to a question I didn't think I could ask.

I stepped through the doorway.

The room was dark, with a panel of lights glowing in a rainbow of colors. Brightly lit squares and circles. Buttons, sliders, and knobs. A control panel. The room hummed with a mechanical buzz. The air circulation system whooshed. There was indistinguishable clicking and ticking. Vibration to my left. A whisper of soft music to my right.

"Edie, you remember Tom?" Hudson said, acknowledging the guy sitting at the control panel. He was one of the guys Hudson had been walking with that day we met on the way to my dorm. "He'll be our captain for this evening's flight."

Captain for this evening's flight? Did I hear him correctly?

"What?" I asked. I didn't have the energy to guess, and knowing Hudson, he would just laugh and tell me it didn't matter.

"This is ground control to Major Tom," Tom said. "Take your protein pills and put your helmet on."

Take your protein pills. What? Where had I heard that before?

"Commencing countdown, engines on," Hudson said, patting his friend on the shoulder before turning to me.

I looked between the two, neither seeming to notice my confusion.

Hudson's hand hovered at the small of my back, urging me toward a door on the opposite side of the room. I could feel the heat from his palm on my exposed skin. I wavered, the darkness of the room ahead sending my senses into high alert.

"If you don't go in, we'll miss our flight," he whispered so close to my ear I could feel his breath. My body responded with goose bumps down both arms.

"Flight?" I asked, stepping into the room. I rubbed my ear against my shoulder, trying to wipe away the shivers his warm breath left on my skin. "What—"

The second room opened into a circular space with a domed ceiling. I knew exactly what he meant now. He *had* said *captain*. He *had* meant *flight*. We were in the planetarium, and we were about to go into outer space.

The room suddenly felt vast and confining at the same time. I couldn't believe he'd brought me here. This was more than anything I had expected. This was so much more. My face was turned to the deep blue expanse above, my mouth hanging open in awe. I was like a little kid, and it felt great.

"Come on," Hudson whispered, reaching for my hand. "The best spot is this way."

I turned my eyes to him, pulling my hand away as his fingertips brushed against my palm.

He moved toward the middle of the room, and I followed. We shuffled between rows, passing dozens of empty chairs. This was our flight. We were the only passengers tonight.

Hudson sat, unbuttoning his tuxedo jacket before crossing his arms and tucking his hands into his sides.

I looked down at him before sitting. I looked at his calm face and bright eyes and kissable lips and didn't know what to say. I'd had a plan.

Go to Paris. Stay in Paris. Don't fall in love. Don't leave with any regrets.

This was not part of the plan.

"It's a bumpy ride. You should probably sit," he said. He reached for my hand again, but I tucked it into my side, crossing my arms as I sat.

"Tom is giving us the whole show," he said, his eyes now on the domed ceiling. I couldn't help but look at him. I'd met him in outer space. We were going into space.

My heart swelled, and I couldn't stop it.

"Hudson, I . . ."

What little light that had filled the room when we entered was suddenly gone. We were plunged into darkness.

He shushed me. "No talking." I could hear the smile in his voice. "Outer space is soundproof, you know. I couldn't hear you if I wanted to."

"Does that rule go for you, too?" I asked, knowing he'd never be able to keep his mouth shut. I smoothed my dress against my legs, wondering how it looked while I was seated. I pressed my hand to my stomach, the belt, feeling for any folding or creasing. It was smooth under my touch.

I felt him turn in his seat toward me. I couldn't see him and he couldn't see me, but I knew he was looking right at me. Seeing me, like he always had. I pressed my hand to my stomach for a different reason now.

"I'm willing to try," he said. A light tinkle of piano started a beat before the lights in the ceiling began to move and shift. "Are you?"

He wasn't talking about keeping his mouth shut, I knew that. He was talking about us, and that was a question I couldn't answer.

"*The universe was born over thirteen and a half billion years ago. . . .*" A deep, smooth male voice spoke softly as the stars moved in an explosion above our heads. "*In the beginning, the universe was just energy—*"

"Can I put my arm around you?" he asked.

I looked at him and his eyes were on me.

"Yes," I said, slouching in the seat. "You can put your arm around me."

He leaned forward as the lights above shifted, pulling off his jacket and laying it on the chair next to him. He slid his arm behind me, his fingers leaving a blazing trail as they skimmed against my bare back. He cupped my shoulder, pulling me in, and I let him.

We watched the show in silence. His arm around me and my head slowly moving toward his shoulder. I wanted so badly to rest my cheek against his chest, explore outer space with him.

"Come here," he whispered. When I looked up he was

already looking at me. I moved closer and he pulled me in. I rested my cheek against his chest, and we watched the universe evolve around us.

The ceiling exploded in colors: blues, greens, and reds. The voice-over calling them protons, neutrons, and electrons. The colors swirled and moved until they were joined, forming bright purple atoms.

The atoms whizzed above our heads. The ceiling was crowded with them, bouncing and colliding until there was no more room for them to move.

"*Regarde les étoiles, comme elles scintillent pour toi et pour tout ce que tu faishe*," he whispered. His lips were moving against my head. "Don't fall asleep."

I yawned, my eyes heavy. It was the first time in days I felt relaxed. "I won't."

"*Menteuse*," he whispered.

"Liar," I said, translating. I smiled against his chest.

"Do you know what happens when you fall asleep in outer space?" he asked as the voice-over talked about stars being born, shining brightly for millions of years and then exploding. The ceiling lit with reds and oranges, then bright white light. The room fell into complete darkness once again.

"No, what?" I asked, feeling his smile against my head.

"You float away." He raised his free arm and wiggled his fingers lazily, floating off into the twinkling stars above us.

I tilted my head to look up at his face. Into his eyes. "Maybe I want to float away."

The lights on the ceiling were cycling through sunrise and sunset. Sunrise. Sunset. The colors, as they lit his face, were incredible. Oranges and pinks turned into yellows and then blues. Then back to oranges and reds, bright blues, pinks and purples, and finally ending on the dark, dark blue night.

"Can I come with you?" he asked.

I looked into his eyes. At his lips. Could he come with me? Or I with him?

My phone buzzed in my pocket. My alarm. It was already midnight. It was already time to face my fate.

I sat up and pulled my phone out at the same time. I could feel Hudson watching me. I took a deep breath and let it out slowly as I clicked the class link.

Seventy-six.

I passed. I passed. Oh my God. I passed.

"I passed," I breathed, pressing my phone to my chest as the night sky lit Hudson's face once again.

"I could have told you that," he said.

"*What*? You made me sit here for an hour, knowing all along I had *passed*?"

"Yeah. I mean, I figured if you wanted to know you would have asked. . . ." He smiled and shrugged, and I was once again torn between punching him and kissing him.

"I might kill you," I started, but stopped as the ceiling moved again. The lights transforming and shifting into something I recognized. The place we'd been headed all along. The place I knew we would end up.

I pointed to the ceiling. "We're here."

Hudson looked up. "Where are we?" His words so faint that had I not been looking at him I would have missed them.

"The entirety of the Milky Way," I said, looking up at the swirl of our galaxy with him. "We made it."

"I know that," he said. "But where are *we*?"

Not the physical where are we, the emotional where are we.

I watched his face. Questioning all that had happened, good and bad. I questioned the future and the right now.

"*I don't want to alarm you, but our galaxy is on an inevitable collision course with the next closest galaxy, Andromeda . . . ,*" the voice-over stated playfully. "*This collision, set to take place within four billion years, will change everything. It will merge the two galaxies into something brand new, something larger, something scientists can't even begin to predict, and nothing will ever be the same. . . .*"

"Galaxies colliding," I said, barely a whisper. That's how I felt when I was with him. I felt like he was unstoppable and I was unstoppable and together that put us on a collision course.

He pulled my hand into his, and I let him. "What?" he asked, leaning into me.

We were two forces that were on a course for inevitable collision. When the Milky Way and Andromeda collide, in four billion years or so, it will be catastrophic, but Hudson and me, could we avoid catastrophe? Could we collide to create something brand new? Something different, but better?

"Wes, I . . . ," I started, but stopped as a shooting star caught my eye. And then another. And then another.

"*Meteor showers, or shooting stars, are often . . .*" The soothing voice interrupted my thoughts.

"Look," I said, pointing to the shooting stars behind him. "Make a wish."

I made a wish as I watched the stars move. And then another as I watched Hudson's face, enchanted by the swirling glow from above.

"Edie," he whispered, his face lit by the meteor shower. "Do you ever see us together again? I just need to know."

"Yes," I breathed, closing my eyes to hold the image of the way a particularly bright shooting star had lit his face. The way the ceiling lit up when the two galaxies collided. The way I felt when we were together.

He cupped my face in his hands. "Yes to what?" I opened my eyes slowly, wanting to cherish and hold this moment forever.

If I could freeze time I would do it right now. In this very moment with this exact boy as the chaos of the universe settled around us.

"*Oui, à tout*," I whispered.

"Yes, to everything," he whispered back, translating for me this time.

Acknowledgments

All the thank-yous to Emily Settle. I don't even know where to start. Thank you for believing in me and my writing. Thank you for giving me a chance. Thank you for loving my book and the characters and their story. You have made me a better writer, and I will be eternally grateful. This has been a long journey, but there is no one else I would have wanted by my side.

Jean Feiwel, Lauren Scobell, Kat Brzozowski, and everyone else on the Swoon Reads team. You are all amazing! Thanks to the Swoon Reads community and to everyone who read and commented on my book. A special thank-you to Sean McMurray for beta reading *MMIOS* when it was in its roughest form and still giving it a thumbs-up, and Moriah Chavis for cheering me on unwaveringly, being my sounding board, and slyly incorporating yourself into my family. You have both been a blessing.

To my reading crew:

Michele Heintz. This book would not have been possible without you. . . . I mean it—don't roll your eyes! You gave Hudson words that I never could have given him. *La vache* times a thousand. *Rendez-vous: au Cosmos*, shall we? Devon Carroll, for reading this book so, so many times. For editing even when I asked you not to. For being my sounding board over and over. For celery stalking and gray barrettes and "I heard spaghetti and meatballs." Lori McCabe. My biggest fan. My number one cheerleader. The only person who has already cleared an entire bookshelf in anticipation of all my future publications.

To my supportive friends:

Thank you to Katie Martel for the German that made Edie swoon and for letting me borrow your name, which you borrowed from Granny. Even though I didn't get a chance to ask her, I'm sure she'd have approved. Twenty-two years and counting. Big love, friend. Julie Bartolotta, I don't think I could have gotten through this without you keeping me sane and talking me through everything, yb. Kate Lloyd. Hi. Love you. Steve Johnson for lending me your name.

Amanda Jones for being my rock. Karole Cozzo, my Big Sis, you have been a godsend, truly. Thank you for answering all my questions, squashing my anxieties, sending me care packages I didn't even realize I needed, and reminding me that we are all in this together. Writing can feel isolating, but you have shown me that it doesn't have to be. I give you all the hearts times a million.

To Sarah Kurland, Jessica Sbiroli, and Megan Mahaney for giving me insight into your experience with having a disability in college.

To my crew at Sitrin: Debbie, Doreen, Brenda, Mayme, Dorothy, and Annie. I love you all dearly for so many reasons. Thank you for your support, all your questions, and all your excitement about my future book signings. Yes, Dorothy, you can certainly be at the front of the line.

To Cheyenne Lyn Foll, for spending so much time looking at my face. You're a saint for putting up with me.

To my awesome family:

Thank you to Jon, my older brother, for teasing me about everything except this. Emily, my sister, who will forever stand up for me to internet trolls. You have been Edie's biggest advocate, and your strength and insight have been invaluable. And Mathew, my brother, for putting up with all my questions about how college students speak, what they wear, how they act, how they text, what they text, etc., etc. Danielle Stolusky, for having the best reaction to the news that my book was chosen and for letting me name a fictional building after you. Jalie Vazquez, for reading all the things I write and for telling me the truth when you don't like something. For laughing at my jokes. For being one of my favorite people on the planet, forever and always. Cheryl Rice, for inspiring me to continue writing, like you have. For teaching me that a writer is someone who writes, a title not exclusive to published authors.

To Andrew, for reading my roughest of drafts, encouraging me to push forward through disappointment, and supporting me. Thank you for believing in me so thoroughly.

To my dad, thank you for teaching me what perseverance looks like. You've shown me dedication and strength through the hardest times, even when giving up seemed easier. To my mom, thank you for giving me the words I needed to make Edie's dress come alive. Thank you for showing me that you can pursue your dreams at any age. Thank you for teaching me how to sew and how to talk with pins in my mouth. Thank you both for always supporting me and encouraging me.

And finally, to Zelda. You have always been my inspiration. You were a brilliant woman, and I miss you every day.

DID YOU KNOW...

readers like you helped to get this book published?

Join our book-obsessed community and help us discover awesome new writing talent.

1 Write it.
Share your original YA manuscript.

2 Read it.
Discover bright new bookish talent.

3 Share it.
Discuss, rate, and share your faves.

4 Love it.
Help us publish the books you love.

Share your own manuscript or dive between the pages at **swoonreads.com** or by downloading the **Swoon Reads app**.

Check out more books chosen for publication by readers like you.